OF MADNESS

Brian Stableford's scholarly work includes *New Atlantis: A Narrative History of Scientific Romance* (Wildside Press, 2016), *The Plurality of Imaginary Worlds: The Evolution of French roman scientifique* (Black Coat Press, 2017) and *Tales of Enchantment and Disenchantment: A History of Faerie* (Black Coat Press, 2019). He has translated more than three hundred volumes from the French, mostly in the genres of *roman scientifique*, *contes de fées* and Romantic and Symbolist fiction. His recent fiction includes the visionary science fiction novel *The Revelations of Time and Space* (2020) and its sequel *After the Revelation* (2021); the last in his long series of "Tales of the Genetic Revolution," *The Elusive Shadows* (2020); and the comedy fantasy *Meat on the Bone* (2021), all published by Snuggly Books.

SNUGGLY BOOKS

brian stableford

BEYOND THE
MOUNTAINS
OF MADNESS

THIS IS A SNUGGLY BOOK

ISBN: 978-1-64525-092-0

BEYOND THE MOUNTAINS OF MADNESS

I

TOM ANDERSLEY was making his way back from the tropical greenhouse to the house when he saw the strange figure limping slowly along the driveway. Bizarre as it was, even seen at a distance, there was something about that uneven gait that triggered a memory in Tom's mind—a memory that had been buried for a long time, covered by many strata of horror, but had somehow remained . . . not fresh, exactly, but *viable*, capable not only of resuscitation but of emotional resonance, of evoking a warm sensation that hybridized nostalgia with fellow-feeling. It was an essentially *good* memory, not just because it was a memory of a good man, but because it was a memory of a better world, the world before the War.

The memory could not be trusted, of course, because the man of whom the approaching figure reminded Tom was long dead, having died even before the Great Catastrophe. He had died a hero. According to the likes of Lord Kitchener, dead heroes had been a penny a gross during the last five years, among whose number Kitchener had figured himself, but Tom had served with the Earl—long before he became one himself—in the Second Boer War and he had known even before 1914 that the real casualties of war were not heroes slain by bullets but men, women and children felled by disease and distress. It had been the same in France, behind the trenches, not only while the bombardments were still thundering, but long after the armistice, given that the so-called Spanish flu had not yet finished gathering its harvest, far more abundant than the deadly reaping of shells and machine-gun fire.

But the man limping slowly along the driveway was obviously walking wounded, evidently not yet beyond help, and whoever he was, it was Tom's duty to help him, to catch him before he fell. So Tom turned aside and went to meet the new arrival, whose particular limp was so strangely reminiscent of one that he had seen before, after his closest friend, then a second lieutenant in the sixth dragoons, had recovered from the bullet wound that had shattered his left femur. When the surgeons had reconnected the fragments—a genuinely heroic endeavor, in Tom's estimation, and a genuine miracle of preservation—the left leg had been an inch shorter than the right, but it hadn't stopped its owner from continuing his military career, with a Victoria Cross to show for his pains. Nor had it stopped him carrying heroism to a new extreme, and becoming, briefly, the most famous and most exemplary of all England's dead heroes. That was before the War, in spite of its relentless propaganda, had obliterated heroism forever . . .

Tom had to abandon the train of thought because it was interrupted by another, when he became convinced, in spite of the absurdity of the notion, that he really had recognized the limp in question, and that the man coming toward him, still fifty or sixty yards away, wasn't dead after all.

Another reputation blown apart, he thought, a trifle churlishly. *It seems that the war isn't going to leave us any intact illusions—although it does make a change to see someone coming back from the dead, when so many hundreds of thousands like him have gone the other way, with equal futility.*

Tom was no stranger to absurd thoughts, and even though it had been nearly a year since the armistice had been signed and the War had been put into cold storage, ready for resumption when the exhausted adversaries had recovered their strength, he still found the supposedly impossible easier to believe than what had previously been taken for granted as plausible . . . but even so, he did not trust himself sufficiently to think that this particular impossibility was actually true, *in Yorkshire*. Anywhere else in the world, perhaps, but if even the Yorkshire wolds no longer counted as an oasis of common sense in a mad world, what hope could there be for humankind?

Tom cast a glance around—not that there could be any true reassurance of the world's normality in the sight of the hillsides, the farms in the valleys with their neatly-cropped post-harvest fields, the ragged sheep on the distant slopes, the fleecy clouds obscuring the summits, or even the house itself; except for the glittering greenhouses, it had all been there for centuries, superficially constant and inviolable, but, in exactly the same way that every single wife who had greeted a husband returned from the War had declared that he wasn't the same man that had gone away, none of it was *the same*, none of it was any longer *normal*, and none of it could prove any intellectual defense against the absurdity of a dead man limping along the drive with a kit-bag slung over his shoulder, crunching the gravel with his ragged and strangely-distended boots.

The limping man seemed to be looking around too, with the same expression, as if he too found everything familiar and yet utterly alien. Lawrence Oates had visited the Andersley estate twice during vacations, while he and Tom were briefly at Eton together, so he could indeed have found it familiar, if . . .

The closer he came, though, the more uncertain Tom became, not just in the negative sense of being less certain that the bizarre figure really was his old friend, but in the more positive sense of being sure that he had to be dreaming, that he had to be hallucinating, that he had lost contact with reality . . . again.

Tom could see the face of the approaching figure now. It was swollen and discolored. In a way, it was definitely not Oates' face, but in another way, it definitely was. In a way, it didn't even seem human, and the way in which it wasn't human wasn't just something that death might have done to it. Tom had seen the faces of many men killed in the trenches and shot in no-man's-land, men who had been gassed, and men who had been blown to Kingdom Come by shell-bursts, but he had never seen a face like that one.

The newcomer was wearing a hooded jacket, with the hood pulled forward as if to keep it concealed from passers-by on the road—although, in truth, he didn't give the impression of having come along the road before turning sideways into the driveway. Although Tom hadn't seen him until he was on the drive, he got the impression from the slow but improbably purposeful stride that the man had been walking for some time in a dead straight line, which implied that he had come across country . . . except that there was nowhere he could have come from for miles in that direction, where ancient slag-heaps left behind by long-abandoned coal-mines had left the soil sterile, unfit for grazing sheep, let alone growing crops.

Is he trying to conceal his face from me? Tom thought, but then answered his question in the negative. Instead, he thought: *He's coming to see me, and he knows that I'll have to see him in order to recognize him. He's already stopped looking round, and he's looking directly at me, exactly as a character in a dream would, and he's about to tip his hood back in order to reveal himself more fully . . .*

The strange figure did exactly that, although the revelatory gesture didn't tell Tom anything that he didn't already know, and didn't disturb his calm of mind in the least. It wasn't a military calm of mind, of course; there was nothing heroic about it. It was the other calm of mind, which a lot of men had brought home from the trenches: the calm of utter resignation, of no longer being able to show concern; the calm that buried all emotion beneath insulating layers of contrived indifference, where even love remained immured, unable to break through.

"Is that really you, Titus?" Tom said, when the other stopped a few feet away. He had never called him Lawrence at Eton, where everyone had a nickname, for form's sake, and in Africa, whether in the West Yorkshires or the Inniskillings, he had been obliged by a different set of rules to address him as *sir*.

"Yes, Linny," said the other, "it's me."

"You're supposed to be dead," Tom objected

"Perhaps I am," he said, proving that the uncertainty cut deeper than appearances. "I have been, at least. How long have I been . . . away?"

"It's been seven years since the newspapers reported your death," Tom informed him. "You really don't know that?"

"No," Oates—or Oates' hallucinatory phantom—replied. "It's 1919, then? Or is it? I'm a trifle . . . confused."

"It's 1919," Tom confirmed. You've missed the War, Soldier."

Tom knew that Scott had called Oates "Soldier" and referred to him routinely in his now-legendary diary as "the Soldier." He had read the version of that diary published by Leonard Huxley in 1913; it was still on the shelves in his study.

"What war?" Oates asked, in all apparent innocence, confirming Tom in the opinion that he had to be hallucinating, that the phantom, no matter how solid it seemed, had to be a figment of a dream.

"*The* War," Tom said. "The War of 1914-18. The Great War, some call it. The War to end War, it was called even before it began, although it surely hasn't. It smashed everything up, irredeemably, but it didn't end anything."

"Against Germany?" Oates enquired.

"Essentially yes," Tom replied, "but in the end, the whole world was on one side or the other, except Switzerland . . . a supposed mountainous island of sanity in a world of madness."

"What was it about?" Oates asked, with the same expression of naivety, which seemed strangely ill-befitting a dead man.

"Nobody knows," Tom said. "It started with the assassination of some Archduke that nobody had ever heard of, in some tinpot nation in the Balkans that nobody had ever heard of, and it just spread, through a network of treaties that were supposed to preserve peace and had the opposite effect. Some people say that it was really about colonies, because we had lots and Germany hadn't, and because Kaiser Bill wanted an empire like King George's, but that's just an attempt to cover up the fact that nobody knows, a quest to find a fugitive atom of supposed reason in a cyclone of madness."

Oates nodded his head—a gesture that made him lurch slightly, and look for an instant as if he might be about to fall over, but he stiffened himself sternly, like a good military man, in spite of the fact that it seemed to Tom that his legs and feet were in an even worse condition than the rest of him.

"*Plus ça change, plus c'est la même chose*," the phantom quoted.

Tom nodded in his turn, although he couldn't quite see the relevance of the remark.

"Are you real, Titus?" he asked, although he didn't suppose that any figment of a dream was likely to confess its own unreality.

Oates put his right hand up to his swollen cheek, as if to test its solidity. "Perfectly real, Linny," he said. "I haven't been well, I suppose, and I've taken a bit of a battering, but I'm recovering, I think. I'll soon be back to my old self. In fact, I still am my old self. You can see that."

Tom could, in fact, see it, but he couldn't quite believe it, yet.

"We'd better get you inside, old man," he said. "You look done in."

"In a minute," the phantom replied. "Let me get my bearings first. You *are* Linny Andersley, aren't you? We were at school together, and the West Yorkshires, and then the dragoons?"

"Yes, we were," Tom said. "You're lucky to have found me. Practically everyone else with whom we were at school or in the dragoons is pushing up poppies in French fields, or rotting at the bottom of the sea. Is your reappearance the beginning of a trend, by any chance? Did the Day of Resurrection arrive while I was tending to my pineapples? I'm still a little deaf—four years of shell-bursts—and it's entirely plausible that I simply didn't hear the call of the Last Trump, but I'm not sure that I'm ready for Judgment yet . . ."

He broke off because Oates had put out his hand to be shaken, as a symbolic renewal of old acquaintance. Tom took it and shook it. It was perfectly solid, not ghostly in the slightest, but it was cold—unnaturally cold, Tom thought—and the fingers were swollen. The cold, Tom thought, could easily have been a subjective impression generated by an association of ideas, and the same could be said of the swelling. Tom had seen frostbitten fingers before, in the trenches, although he supposed that the Antarctic chill must have been far worse than anything France could muster in the dead of winter.

Tom felt a couple of tears forming in the corners of his eyes, and he couldn't stop them brimming over, although he wasn't entirely sure what had occasioned them. His emotions had been unhinged for quite some time, and these certainly weren't the first tears he had shed since coming home, but that didn't alter the fact that blubbing was conduct unbecoming of an officer and an Old Etonian, whatever the reason for the disturbance might be. Unfortunately, Tom had lost track of "becoming" somewhere in northern France, even before the Front was fully formed, and he had not found it in all his subsequent postings, including the last, when he had been deliberately sent southwards to what was notionally a quieter posting, in order to recuperate from exhaustion. It hadn't turned out that way, and he hadn't made any progress since in catching up with becoming. That was one of the reasons why he was unready for Judgment, although not the most important.

"It's good to see you, Linny," said Oates. "I haven't seen a half-way friendly face for a long time—seven years, apparently—and you have no idea how welcome yours is, in spite of..." He stopped, and his puffy face... more frostbite, Tom assumed... frowned awkwardly.

"I'm doing my best," Tom told him, although he was sure that Oates hadn't been criticizing the partiality of his welcoming expression. Nobody had called Tom "Linny" for ten years; the last time he'd seen Oates was in 1909, and Oates been the last habitual user of the Etonian nickname. He added: "How on Earth did you get here, Titus?"

Oates' physiognomy shifted then, in a very peculiar fashion, which Tom was hesitant to describe as an "expression." It was disconcerting to look at, and Tom couldn't imagine what sort of twinge might have caused the reaction. *This isn't one of my normal nightmares, he thought. It ought to be a pleasant dream, but I'm not entirely sure that I prefer it.* He wasn't serious. He had already abandoned the hypothesis that Oates might be a hallucination. He was real: impossible, but real.

All that Oates said in reply, though, was: "I walked."

That wasn't good enough. The limping man didn't look as if he could have made it all the way along the driveway, let alone all the way from Driffield or anywhere further away.

"Where the Hell from?" Tom demanded. "Antarctica?"

The twitch in the phantom's features recurred, worse the second time, and Tom felt certain that many a man would have found the sight of that change alarming. Tom didn't have any reaction of fear, but he did feel guilty about having provoked such a response. Something was evidently wrong with Oates, akin to what recent jargon called "shell shock," even though he had apparently missed every one of the War's terrible shells.

Tom had seen numerous cases of shell shock—probably more than poor Helen, who had seen more than her fair share—and he knew that it was unkind to press victims to talk about the things they were blotting out. He was in sympathy with the now-prevailing opinion that it was necessary to be patient, and let the buried topics resurface again in their own time.

"Ultimately," Oates replied, uncertainly, screwing up his puffy face as if he were striving to remember, "but not directly. I was underground more recently, I think."

"In a mine?" said Tom, incredulously. There were, in fact, abandoned mines within what he would consider walking distance of the manor, in the direction from which Oates might have come if his limp along the drive had been extrapolated in a straight line from a hike across country, but Oates did not look as if he were in any condition to have walked as far as the nearest one—and how, in any case, would he have got out if he had been in one? The last of the active pits had closed in the 1870s, and those that were still uncapped were waterlogged death-traps.

"Probably," said Oates.

It made no sense, but Tom only thought: *So what?* He didn't have to understand—not yet, at least. Oates was here, in the manor's grounds, and as a host, as well as a friend, Tom had obligations.

"Come inside, old man," he said. "We'll go into my study while I take a look at your feet, and I'll pour you a stiff brandy. I'll order a pot of tea, too. Once we've got you warmed up, you can fill me in."

Oates still seemed uncertain, as if he were having second thoughts about having come, although he had evidently been heading for the house, and there was no conceivable reason for him to have been doing that except to see his old friend.

"I'm not sure I can do that, Linny," Oates said. "I'm having a little trouble remembering. Seven years, you say?"

"A little more than seven years," Tom confirmed. "Can't you remember where you've been, Titus?"

"Vaguely," Oates replied, "but it's very confused . . . like a fever-dream." He looked around again. "Yes," he said, "all this is real. I remember it . . . those hills, this world . . . even the house . . . but not the hothouses. They're . . . new."

"Yes," said Tom. "They're a lot bigger than the ones we had last time you were here. Those were where the gardener planted out seeds that needed protection . . . flowers, mostly, and a few fruits. I concentrate on fruits—trees, mostly . . . trees that don't normally grow in Yorkshire."

"A *jardin d'acclimation*," Oates said, his face clearing slightly, becoming noticeably less hideous in so doing. He had remembered the term from Eton, where Tom had told him about the various French *jardins d'acclimation*, scattered equivalents of Kew, in which dozens of amateur hobbyists had continued that particular project of colonialism . . . almost all gone now, of course, murdered by the Catastrophe.

"That's right, Titus," Tom said, perfectly prepared to humor his guest while the latter was still confused,

18

eager to help him as a comrade should. He had lost a lot of comrades, the help he owed them and had tried to provide for them having proved futile far too often. Perhaps this was an opportunity for a measure of redemption. "My project is like the work done at Kew, but on a much smaller scale. We visited the Temperate House there once, remember. This is tiny by comparison, but it's the best I could do, and it's not unimpressive, for the Yorkshire wolds. It's my . . . distraction." He didn't want to say "hobby" because it was much, much more than that, and he didn't want to say "obsession," because he wanted to sound completely rational, as an officer and a gentleman should, in spite of the fact that so few of them were.

"They must have known that," Oates muttered, talking to himself rather than Tom.

"Who must have known it, Titus?"

"The barrel-boys . . . but I don't know how. I shouldn't try to wonder. When you try to wonder in a dream whether anything makes sense, you sometimes wake up. I remember that, although I remember trying . . . in dreams within the dream . . . and it didn't work. This time, I don't want to wake up, if this is just another dream . . . but I have the strangest feeling that it isn't. *Are* you real, Linny . . . really real?"

I sometimes wonder that myself, Tom thought, but he knew that it would be the wrong thing to say.

"Yes, Titus," he said, although he knew that it ought to be a lie. "I'm real; it's all real." And as he said it he became utterly convinced that it wasn't a lie: that Lawrence Oates was really standing there, on his driveway, slightly unsteadily but very solidly. He was in a pretty bad way—a very bad way, to judge by appearances—but he was alive. His costume was odd—more a caricature of army battle-dress than an actual uniform, and devoid of insignia of rank—and the kit-bag slung over his shoulder wasn't army issue either, but the cloth had the appearance of being real cloth, designed for warmth, and the oversized boots looked sturdy enough, albeit badly scuffed.

Tom thought that it was time to insist. He reached out and took Oates' arm. "We've got to get you inside, old man," he said. "You need to sit down, and then to lie down. I need to take a look at your legs. If you've walked from the old mines, they can't be as bad as all that, but they need looking at. I've had some medical training, during the War, and Helen was a nurse for more than two years. We can make you comfortable, and we have medical supplies. Please, Titus."

"Yes, of course," Oates replied, vaguely, "that's why I'm here. But Linny . . ."

"What is it, Titus?"

Oates seemed to be struggling with a thought that he could not quite pin down.

"It . . . might not be a good idea to let me in."

"Why not, Titus?"

"Because . . ." The struggle was still continuing. Eventually Oates whispered: "Because you don't know where I've been."

"That's true, Titus," Tom admitted, "but I expect that you'll tell me in your own time. For now, the important thing is that you're here, and you need my help.

So come on in, for God's sake, and take the weight of your feet. Unless you'd like to tell me beforehand where it is that you've spent the last seven years . . . ?"

Tom immediately regretted having added the final sentence, because Oates' face twitched again, taking on a mask suggestive of strange horror.

Tom had seen a great many horrified expressions in his time; if anyone had asked, he would have assured them that he had seen everything that human physiognomy had to offer in that particular line—but it seemed that he hadn't.

Oates was still struggling with himself, but eventually, he managed to whisper: "Beyond the Mountains of Madness"—which didn't seem to Tom to be very informative. So far as he could remember, he had never heard of the Mountains of Madness—but then, he had never heard of Sarajevo, so far as he could remember, before Archduke Ferdy had been shot there by some crazy Serb, and look what had come of that.

"That's all right, old man," he said. "Personally, I've been beyond the Trenches of Madness, but I'm home again now, and so are you. Let's go into the study and see whether we can't pick up a few of the pieces, shall we?"

Oates capitulated. "If you say so, Linny," he said. "You're the one man in the world I can trust. My God, it's good to see you . . . you have no idea . . ."

"Actually, my old friend," Tom replied, honestly, "I think I do. It's good to see you too, old man. Come inside, and let's have a drink, and a chat about old and better times."

II

TOM guided Oates into the house, going in through the side door, where they were less likely to be seen by the servants. Not that the servants would make any comment, and probably wouldn't even feel any particular alarm at the sight of a man in a bad way—they had seen plenty of others, after all—but Tom couldn't help feeling an urge to maintain secrecy for a little while, if possible. He wanted to introduce Oates to Helen first of all, if only to make sure that he wouldn't disappear in a puff of sulfurous smoke as soon as he was confronted with virtue incarnate.

Tom took Oates into his study, and closed the door behind them quietly. He offered him the best armchair, because it was in a more convenient position relative to the desk than the sofa, and Tom wanted to be at the desk, where he could more readily pose as a scientist, a man of the utmost reason.

Oates seemed very glad indeed to be able to sit down. Quite apart from the limp, his feet now seemed to be giving him a lot of pain. It didn't make any sense to Tom that he could have walked far, but how else could he have arrived? The manor didn't get many visitors any more—hardly any, in fact, apart from tenants with problems and the occasional awkward duty visit from the vicar who felt obliged to support Helen in her dire misfortune of being married to a notorious atheist. If Oates had been an ordinary visitor from further afield he would probably have come via the railway station at Driffield and then taken a taxi . . . but Tom only had to look at his face to know that he was beyond that kind of mundane practicality.

Wherever Oates had come from, he concluded, and however he came to be here, he must have done it by extraordinary means, probably with an extraordinary purpose. That did not make him any less welcome. Even if he really had stepped out of the land of the dead, from a darkness that was not the mundane obscurity of an abandoned mine—which actually seemed to Tom to be the likelier possibility, in his present state of mind, however implausible it might seem—it did not make him any less welcome. Even if he really was dead, and had spent the last seven years in a supernatural Underworld, he was a friend

And he can't possibly have been in Hell, if there were any such place, Tom thought. *He's an Old Etonian, and a hero.*

Tom poured Oates a large brandy and handed it to him. Then he went to the door, stepped into the corridor, and shouted for Janet, the housekeeper. When she appeared at the end of the corridor, he said: "I'm in the study, Janet; could you have Maggie make a large pot of tea, please? Knock and leave it outside the door, will you—I don't want to be disturbed. And put two cups on the tray, would you?"

Janet, a stout Yorkshirewoman who had been in service at the manor for twenty years, showed not the slightest flicker of surprise at the eccentric request. Tom had had a reputation for eccentricity even when he was "Master Tom," before Eton and enlistment, while the Old Earl was still alive. Since he had come back from the war, leaving his father and two older brothers dead in France, the general opinion among the servants was that he was "doolally tap," a term which had made its way to Yorkshire from India in his grandfather's day. The Old Earl had been a stalwart of the Raj for many years, and although he had only spent a few years of his retirement ruling the manor with an iron fist, his over-bearing influence had contrived to permeate its culture thoroughly and to corrupt all the servants, from the old butler down. Hollis, the old butler, was dead now, like the Old Earl, and had similarly not been replaced, but his ghost still haunted Janet, in her actions and her opinions.

Tom returned to his desk and sat down.

"You have no idea how good it is to see a friendly face," Oates said, apparently convinced that there were a great many things about which Tom could have no idea.

"It's good to see you, too, Titus," Tom said. He had no shortage of friendly faces around him—loving faces, even—but there seemed to be some kind of strange barrier between them and him; he had expected it to disappear, with time, as life reverted to normal after the War, but it had only diminished slightly, if at all, and its long duration made it seem more tangible, perhaps insurmountable. Dead or alive, Titus was from a different world: an old world, a lost world, where there had been no such boundaries, and he was a reminder of that freer world.

Perhaps, Tom thought, Oates had been sent by a remorseful Providence to help him reconnect with civilized values, decency, and a kinder order of things—but he dismissed the thought, unworthy of a man of science, who knew perfectly well that there was no Providence, and that if there had been, it surely would not have been remorseful.

He poured himself a brandy as generous as the one he had given Oates, which Oates had not yet touched, presumably waiting politely for his host to join him. It was the last of the Cognac that Tom had brought back "from the other side of the pond," but it was not the last physical reminder of the Inferno he had endured there that was still lingering in his immediate environment, even though his medals had been confined to a drawer, his uniforms to a trunk in the attic and his service revolver, after a sojourn in his bedside cabinet, to the tropical greenhouse. He was not one for keeping mementos, and he had even banished the Old Earl's trophies and panoplies from the study, although Janet kept the least moth-eaten of the animal-heads on ostentatious display in the drawing room, and took care to furbish the spearheads, following precedents set by Hollis.

"I'm glad you came through it, Linny," Oates said, when he had relaxed deliberately and had taken a swig of the brandy. "The war you mentioned, I mean."

"Somebody had to," Tom told him, a trifle churlishly. "Like Voltaire, I couldn't see the necessity, but it wasn't yet time for the world to end, so some of us had to be left alone to carry on. Yorkshire would never have forgiven us if the earldom had died and the manor had been sold at auction to some incomer from London. I was always reckoned to be the fool of the family, and unlikely to bring the glory to the Andersley name that the Old Earl had, but for want of anything else, I'll just have to do."

"But you're anything but a fool, Linny," Oates said. "You're a true intellectual, a scientist, much cleverer than a duffer like me."

"This is the East Riding," Tom remarked. "Not a lot of difference between intellectuals and fools, in the eyes of the common Yorkshireman. Why don't you slip your boots off and let me take a look at your feet?"

"In a minute," the other said. "This brandy's good. It's a long time since I had a drink . . . a real drink. It's . . . warming."

Tom was still looking at Oates' trousers. "Is that a bloodstain on the thigh?" he asked. "That's where you were shot in '06. Has the wound opened up again?"

"It did for a while, in the Antarctic," Oates said. "That imbecile Scott hadn't made sufficient dietary provisions in the food dumps, and scurvy caused the scar tissue to break down. But it's much better now. That stain is . . . I don't know how old, but not recent. I suppose that I don't look too good, but believe me, I'm better than I was. I'm on the mend."

"That's good," Tom said. "Perhaps I ought to ask Janet to have the fire made up . . . ?"

"Not on my account," said Oates, dismissively. "I'm used to the cold. That last blizzard on the Ross shelf, and then . . ." He stopped suddenly, visibly repelling the memory. Deliberately, his gaze scanned the bookshelves. "Forgive me saying so, Linny," he said, "but this is where you always belonged. I don't say you weren't a good soldier, because you were, but . . . well, it wasn't where you belonged. I used to think that it was my fault that you followed me into the army, and that I should have stopped you."

"Nonsense," said Tom. "It was you who followed me into the West Yorkshires, and then we transferred to the Iniskillings together in order to stay together. I didn't have any choice about enlisting, any more than I had any choice about Eton—the Old Earl's whims were irresistible—but it worked out well for me, since I met you. You're quite right about me not being cut out for soldiering, though. I was glad to resign the commission—but the resignation didn't count, once the War started. Poor soldier or not, everyone had to . . . *do his bit*. My father was a far better soldier than I could ever be, and so were Jack and Hal, but . . . perhaps that's why they fell and I didn't . . . too soldierly for their own good, too proud to duck and too slow to run away. There are times when it's healthy to have a little rabbit in you."

"No, Linny," Oates said, "I didn't mean that you were a bad soldier. You weren't. I was with you in action in Africa, in the bloodiest of circumstances, and there was no one better . . . it's just that it wasn't your true vocation. The army was where I belonged, though . . . far more so than in the Antarctic with that cretin Scott. I should have been in your War instead of . . ."

Again he stopped dead. His features twisted again, but Tom couldn't tell what thought had occasioned the grimace. Oates' face did not have the capacity at present for readable expression; the army, of course, had tried to train that out of him, but Tom doubted that it could have succeeded to the extent that now afflicted it. The War might have, but he had missed the War. *Lucky sod*, Tom couldn't help thinking—although, looking at Oates sagging in the armchair, with his face an utter mess, he couldn't help feeling that perhaps Oates hadn't been lucky at all.

"Take off your boots, Titus," he repeated. "Let me have a look at your feet."

"Not yet, Linny," Oates replied. "Let me pull myself together first. I have a slight suspicion that my toes might come away with my socks, even though they're better than they were. They could have done, when . . . but they didn't. I'm not as bad now, but I'm not yet convinced that the danger is over. I need to finish pulling myself together. Give me a minute, will you?"

"Of course," Tim said. "Take all the time you need."

There was a brief double rap on the door. Tom couldn't hear any footsteps moving away along the corridor, but he assumed that the absence was a testament to Janet's discretion, not evidence that she was still hovering outside, listening in.

He was right; when he opened the door to pick up the tray, there was no longer anyone in the corridor. He brought the tray in and set it down on the desk. There were two cups, as requested. He poured tea into the cups.

"Milk?" he said to Oates. "Fresh from the udder this morning, I don't doubt. The biscuits might be a slightly older vintage, but they'll be the produce of this year's harvest—which is more than can be said for anything the army ever served us."

Oates accepted the biscuit as well as the milk in his tea. He sipped with the kind of polite delicacy that could have passed muster in Harrogate, let alone the wolds.

"That's good too," he said. "I'd forgotten . . ."

"You're at home now, Titus," Tom assured him. "When I've had a look at your foot, I'll show you to your room, and I'll ask Janet to have a hot bath drawn. We don't dress for dinner, so I'll ask her to put out one of my lounge suits with clean linen. It won't quite fit, given the height difference, but it'll be better than those fatigues you have on . . . unless, of course, you have something in your kitbag."

Oates looked down at the kitbag, which he had laid down beside the chair.

"No," he said, "I don't think it has any clothes in it." He paused, as if weighing up that assertion, and then continued: "I've brought you something, Linny," he said. "I need your help. You might be the only man in England who can help—I think that's why I'm here."

"You think?" Tom queried. "You don't know?"

After a moment's thought, Oates said: "Yes, that's why I'm here. I need your help."

"If it's a matter of money . . ."

"Don't be ridiculous, Linny," said Oates. "I could have got that elsewhere . . . at least, I think I could, if I could face the family . . . . . which I'm really not up to, at present. I knew that you'd be able to look at me without flinching, after the things we saw in Africa back in '07, but . . . well, I don't exactly have a face that a mother could love, at present, do I?"

Evidently, Tom concluded, there had been reflective surfaces of some sort wherever Oates had been, and enough light to look into them. "But you'll have to let her know that you're not dead, won't you?" he said, slightly shocked for the first time—which seemed odd, because he had assumed that he was no longer subject to shock where matters of social nicety were concerned. Oates' judgment had been harsh, but possibly true— but whether his mother could love him or not, Tom, thought, she was still his mother.

"Perhaps I will," Oates said, "if I can convince myself, but not yet. Let me see, first, whether I can . . . recover a little more of my old self."

Tom lost patience. "What the hell happened to you, Titus?" he said, unable to contain himself any longer even though he knew that it might be necessary as well as polite, if Oates really was suffering some kind of trauma. "According to Scott's journal, you were completely done in. 'I'm just going out for a walk, chaps,' you're supposed to have said, or words to that effect. 'I may be gone a while!'—and then off you went into the blizzard, trying to give the other three a chance of making it to the next supply dump. You know, I suppose, that they *didn't* make it?"

"I know," Oates said. This time he actually tried to grimace, but he was better at that when he wasn't trying. "I wish I really had said that," he replied. "Just that, I mean. I was so angry with Scott, because I thought he'd killed us all with his casual recklessness and lousy planning. I couldn't stand the sight of him any longer, and I let him have it . . . not for the first time. I can hardly blame him for leaving the rest out, mind, and I suppose I ought to be grateful to him for deleting the expletives—but no, what I actually said was a good deal less worthy, and there was more pique than self-sacrifice in my storming out. Typical of Scott to put a different slant on it, always thinking of appearances, and writing his journal for posterity."

"But you did go out into the blizzard—to die?"

"Yes, I went out into the blizzard, to die. I didn't intend to go far—hell, my toes were all frostbitten and that old gunshot wound from '06 had opened up again because of the scurvy. I didn't think I'd get a hundred yards—but it wouldn't have been fair to Birdy and Ed just to lie down and die on the doorstep, so I figured that the least I could do was take a header into the nearest crevasse."

"But you didn't?"

"Of course I did—but it wasn't easy. You've no idea how difficult it is to locate a crevasse in a whiteout when you're actually trying to find one, even one that you've spotted on the way in. I seemed to be stumbling around for hours, although it couldn't have been more than a few minutes. I found it, though, and I stepped into it. I remember thinking that at least I'd find out whether there really was water under the ice, or whether I'd simply hit the sea-bed, all the water above it having been turned to a brine lollipop."

31

"And did you—find water, I mean?"

"I can't remember. I suppose I must have lost consciousness before the slide stopped. I didn't recover it for quite some time, and when I did . . . well, I wasn't at the bottom of a crevasse. I thought that I was dead, but dreaming. I probably was . . . am . . . except that I don't quite feel dead any more, or that I'm dreaming. Not that I'm saying that I couldn't have dreamed about you, and the brandy, and the tea, because I'm fairly sure that I dreamed all of those things at some point . . . absolutely certain, in fact, because if I hadn't talked in my sleep about you, they wouldn't have sent me here, would they?"

"Wouldn't they?" Tom countered.

"I don't think so," Oates said, after taking another swig of brandy and a sip of tea. "I'm on a mission, Linny."

"What mission?" Tom asked—although, once again, it was more a defensive parry than a matter of taking the initiative.

Oates ignored the question, seemingly searching his memory for another item. After a pause, and more tea, he said: "I'm not sure whether or not this is my first trip back to the world . . . a trip that isn't just a dream, that is. I think I might have served before."

"Served?" Tom queried.

"As a pair of eyes, probably . . . a spotter, or a spy. I'm . . . well, I'd trust you with my life, Linny, and have, in the past . . . but I'm not entirely sure that you can trust me any longer, even though they can't actually *control* me. I'd like to think so, but . . . I can't entirely trust myself, and I'm not entitled to ask you for your trust ... or even your hospitality. They won't like it if I don't go through with it, but ..." His face contorted yet again, as if he had spoken the truth and as if they were demonstrating, by some means, that they did not, in fact, like him telling Tom that he could not be trusted.

"Who are *they*?" Tom interrogated.

"The barrel-boys," said Oates, as if that were somehow an answer.

Tom took the discussion back slightly. "If you weren't at the bottom of the crevasse in the Ross ice-shelf," he said, quietly, "where were you, Titus, when you woke up?"

"Good question," said Oates. "I'm a little confused at the moment, but I think I might be able to work it out, given time. Where have I been these last seven years? Not under the ice ... not under the ice over the sea, at any rate. I think ... I presume ... that they took me into the labyrinth, perhaps only to the continent ... the far side, where the ice is so thick that it buries mountains ... the Mountains of Madness ... but perhaps far beyond, in strange directions ..."

He paused for thought, and then went on: "The Antarctic hasn't always been cold, you know. It's in an Ice Age now, but in its day ... it's been almost tropical. Has the Earth shifted on its axis, do you think? I think it might have done, in spite of the law of the conservation of angular momentum. Perhaps the crust can slip over the mantle and the core. Are there doorways in time as well as in space? I think there might be. At any rate, wherever I was, I was in some sort of dream-space

. . . but the dream was real. Physically, perhaps I have been under the ice, deep frozen . . . but mentally . . . mentally, I think I've traveled further than Odysseus, and wherever I went . . . I was there—really there.

"They can do that. They can do a great deal . . . but they're not gods, not even demigods. In their way, they're weak, so weak that they have to work in sly and mysterious ways . . . and they don't get many opportunities, as you can imagine, based in the Antarctic. They can travel, but the labyrinth is . . . difficult of negotiation even without the minotaurs . . ."

"Minotaurs?" Tom couldn't help querying.

"Just another nickname. I had to give them nicknames in my mind, Linny, because they didn't have names and I didn't have descriptions. I didn't mean by *minotaur* a man with a bull's head, I just meant something that lives in a labyrinth. Some of them are big, as massive as trains on the London Underground, but most of them are tiny. It's a bad nickname, I suppose, but it's all I could come up with . . . God, it hurts to think when you don't have words to think with; it's as if my brain were in a vice. Drop it for a while, will, you, Linny. I'll tell you everything, when I can . . . everything I know, that is, but it isn't much. For now, my head hurts worse than my feet . . . but I think you're right, Linny . . . that I need to take my boots off, whatever the risk. Come on Soldier, buck up, old man . . ."

His voice faded away, but not his scowl. It seemed to Tom that Scott's voice and the nickname that Scott had invented might be haunting his friend—but only in illusion. Scott was definitely dead. The barrel-boys,

34

whoever or whatever they were, hadn't been able to do anything for him, nor for Wilson and Bowers.

Tom was at a loss to understand. The Scott expedition had been a long way out on the Ross Shelf, he knew, heading for the next dump of food and fuel, but the weather had been too bad; they couldn't travel fast enough, and poor Oates had been slowing them down, hence his self-sacrificial action. It made sense that his body had never been found, given that he had deliberately stepped into a crevasse—but what, in that case, did his talk about mountains mean? If mysterious rescuers had indeed found him in the crevasse, and kept him alive somehow, where could they have taken him and how? Surely not to the slopes of Mount Erebus, even though the vicinity of an active volcano was likely to be the only place on the continent where a certain amount of warmth was to be found.

Were there really mountains buried in ice elsewhere on the continent? Tom wondered. Probably. Almost certainly—but what would be the point of taking Oates to a buried mountain, and how could it have been done? Perhaps there really was an underworld beneath the continent, beneath the mountains . . . a labyrinth, complete with minotaurs of various dimensions. Perhaps . . .

"You're not making much sense, I'm afraid, Titus," Tom told his friend—but not resentfully. The world had stopped making sense in '16, on day one of the slaughter on the Somme, and it wasn't about to start again any time soon. Tom couldn't honestly say that he'd become accustomed to it, or even that he'd learned to live with it, but he knew that whether you learned to live with it or not, you still had to go through it, with or without any hope of getting to the other side.

Oates had not yet made any move to take off his boots, even though he had accepted the necessity, on principle. "I know I'm not making much sense," he said sadly. "I'm not even sure that there's any sense to be made, but if there is, I can't make it yet. Give me time, Linny. I need time, and I haven't had much for quite some time . . . although that doesn't make any sense either, come to think about it. Forgive me."

"There's nothing to forgive, Titus," said Tom, mildly. "Relax. You're safe now . . . as safe as you can be. You're at home. Let me take a look at your feet, please. I'll pull your boots off, if you'll let me. I've done it before, re-member, more than once."

Whether Oates remembered or not, the suggestion did not win his immediate consent; he had other things on his mind, although he seemed to wish that he hadn't.

"I've brought you some seeds, Linny," he said. "I need you to grow them for me, if you can. They'll need a greenhouse, mind—as hot and humid as you can make it—and some very special soil, but you've got the greenhouse, haven't you, and a ready source of animal blood? The hothouses are much bigger and better than when I was here before, and although I was walking on barren ground, I could see sheep and cattle in the distance."

"The benefits of inheritance," Tom observed, brusquely. "I own a few cattle, a lot of sheep, and an abattoir. What kind of seeds, Titus? Fruit trees?"

Tom suspected as he said it that it was a silly sug-gestion. He grew fruit trees in the tropical house; that was a specialty of his—but he knew that Oates couldn't possibly be bringing him pineapples, breadfruit or bananas from the Antarctic.

"No," said Oates. "That is, I don't know, exactly . . . but I'm pretty sure they're not fruit. I'm pretty sure that they're not really plants, in fact."

"They can't really be seeds, then."

Oates sighed. "Maybe not. Maybe they're eggs that just need soil and blood for incubation. Most likely they're unnamable, because we have nothing like them, and we'll have to improvise nicknames. But I can't help thinking of them as seeds—a duffer, remember, at least in botanical matters."

"Seeds from the Mountains of Madness?"

"No, seeds from beyond them."

"Vampire seeds? Seeds that need *blood* in order to grow?"

"Yes. They'll also need minerals . . . exactly what might take a bit of figuring out, with a little trial-and-error, once I've given you the gist. They knew there was no point getting me to plant them myself, or taking them to any common-or-garden gardener. They knew that it would need an expert touch to bring them to maturity, someone used to supervising a *jardin d'acclimation.* And they need them brought to maturity, Linny. I don't know why, but they do. They need them to be *ready* as soon as possible."

"And they think that I'm qualified to help you—because they plucked my name and that term from your dreams?

"That's right," he said, unsurprised by the deduction, although it wasn't a conclusion to which any commonsensical Yorkshireman would normally have leapt. Clearly, Tom thought, the two of them were entering into a kind of conspiracy of delusion. It wasn't exactly Eton and the Transvaal all over again, but Eton and the Transvaal probably had something to do with the effect. At any rate, there was no point in telling Oates that he could and should have gone to Kew. Oates didn't know anyone at Kew, and even though he had visited the Temperate House and admired it as a masterpiece of Victorian architecture, there was no reason why he should have dreamed about it, whereas dreaming about his school days and days of comradeship in southern Africa would have been unavoidable. Oates had chanced to become acquainted with "Linny" Andersley when the two of them were young and innocent, and again when they had lost what remained of their youth and innocence fighting the Boers and the blacks, not knowing that the sorry mess in question was just a tune-up for the real Big Show. If he had also dreamed about seeds, what other connection could his dormant mind possibly have made?

"You're lucky I went back to my hobby," Tom said. "Helen says that I'm not the same man that I was when I went away, and believe me, she's in a position to know. On the other hand, Janet would probably judge that I'm more myself than I was before, that I'm simply able to let my old doolally obsessions run free now that I've got the title, the house and the money. The title wasn't on the cards, of course, when you knew me before. Jack was the heir apparent, Hal the reserve. I was the idle afterthought, only fit for the army or the church—or to be a dilettante dabbling in science, although father, taking up where grandfather left off, wouldn't even have included that in his list of possibilities. The Old Earl, in spite of being devout in his fashion, never looked beyond the army. But the war changed everything, and the army took us all, and I'm really not the same man as I was before, according to my title. Not that anybody hereabouts actually thinks of me as Lord Andersley, even on the estate. I'm still the eccentric child who likes trees. I've only been to the House once—London is more than two hundred miles away."

"Luck has nothing to do with it," Oates said. "It was always a vocation. I could see that. You're the only man I know who ever reconciled himself to being forced to join the army by telling himself that it would help to further his studies in botany."

"It wasn't an original idea," Tom told him, ruefully. "There were notable precedents, in France. There were also Frenchmen who went into the church and became missionaries simply in order to further their studies in botany. In Britain it used to be the navy, following the inspiration of the great Joseph Banks and poor William Bligh, men who knew how important the science might be to the project of world colonization, to the project of growing food in places where native vegetation was inadequate to the economics of the human diet: the only true conquest of the world. Not that it did either of them any good in the long run—or any of us. All that our great ecological adventure achieved, in the end, was to spread our war worldwide."

"Ecological adventure?" Oates queried.

"New jargon," Tom explained. "Ecology is the study of organisms in relation to their environment. What the French call *acclimation*—the strategic attempt to adapt organisms to new environments by selectively breeding new strains—is its active branch. It's not just a matter of cultivating exotic flowers any more, or of breeding crops adapted for transplantation to new continents; it's more exploratory, delving down into the . . . oh, damn it, Titus: *seeds?* Are you *serious?* You've come back from the land of the dead to ask me to plant some *seeds* for you?"

"I'm not actually sure that I've come all the way back," Oates said, reaching down to massage his calves through the cloth of his trousers, "but yes, that was the reason that they sent me back, and the price of their contriving the journey through the labyrinth . . . the price of my coming back from the dead, if I really am back, and back to England, if . . . "

"Oh, this is England all right," Tom interjected. "Unrecognizable, in the faces and hearts of its people, if not in its landscape, but England nevertheless. Bringing the seeds to me was the price you had to pay for your ticket back to Blighty, then?"

"That's right. And growing them is the price you'll have to pay, if you're willing, to keep me here . . . for a while," Oates said. "I need to ask you to do that, Linny . . . but it might not be a good idea. It might be dangerous."

"Why?"

"I don't know, Linny. I have no idea what the seeds might become."

Tom considered the puzzle for a few moments. They had both emptied their glasses and the tea cups. There was still brandy in the bottle and tea in the pot, but Tom didn't attempt to replenish the glasses or the cups, for the moment.

Eventually, he said: "If you hadn't brought me the seeds, or if I refuse to grow them . . . they'll take you back to wherever you've been these last seven years?"

"Probably," Oates said. "There isn't exactly a formal agreement."

"And what are *they*, exactly . . . the barrel-boys, that is?"

"Exactly?" Oates echoed. "That, I don't know. Not human, probably not of this earth."

"Like Wells' Martians?"

"Probably from much further away than that. It makes my head hurt to think about it . . . I think I might be able to explain, in time, but . . . not unless and until we make some progress with the seeds. All I can tell you, for the moment, is that they need to figure out how to grow the seeds in what, to them, is alien soil. That's why they . . . allowed me to come back. I had to bring the seeds to you."

"To me? Specifically to me?"

"Yes. I'm sorry, Linny—I might have sung your praises a little more loudly than was necessary, in my dream."

"That's understandable," Tom opined. "Flattering, in fact. If the dead can dream, they must be very vulnerable to nostalgia. If they're looking to establish a *jardin d'acclimation* in Yorkshire, because it's too cold at the

41

South Pole, I suppose this is the logical place to come . . . to send you, that is . . . once they learned from you about my ambition to develop one of my own."

"Yes," said Oates, nodding his head, "that's it, exactly." But he did not give the impression of being pleased to have clarified the matter. He was still massaging his calves, and it seemed to Tom that a shudder ran through him from head to toe, like a strange chill.

Tom didn't want to press him any further, while he obviously wasn't ready, as yet, to specify who, or what, the barrel-boys might be, and what they might want, above and beyond gardening advice. It was something that Oates couldn't talk about . . . yet. Tom could sympathize with that, entirely. There were things that he couldn't talk about, yet, even to Helen . . . particularly to Helen. He understood what it was like to feel that one needed time in order to creep up stealthily on certain matters of experience that one knew that one would have to deal with eventually, but not without preparing the psychological ground very carefully,

At Eton, and in the dragoons, he and Oates had been an odd couple, unlikely friends—but they had bonded nevertheless, more tightly than any randomly-selected pair of Old Etonians or veterans of Kitchener's African crusade. It was, in a strange fashion, perfectly natural that Titus, exiled from the world but offered a chance to reconnect with it, would reach out to Tom Andersley. And it was perfectly natural that Tom would welcome him with open arms—arms that he had not been able even to open fully for Helen or Mercy, although he loved them more than life itself—in spite of Oates' sinister warnings of untrustworthiness or danger.

Tom remembered what the enlisted men used to say, with a ritual shrug of the shoulders, when things at the Front became too absurd: "We don't have to understand it; we just have to do it." They had left understanding to the officers. A bad move, as it turned out. What was it that Ludendorff was rumored to have said about lions led by donkeys? The poor donkeys hadn't understood at all—and even as a lowly captain, which was as far as Tom's battlefield promotions had extended, he couldn't dodge the responsibility of having been part of that dismal failure: for the fact that, because he and his kind hadn't understood, the poor sods who only had to go and do it had only gone and done it, and had died without the slightest hope of understanding. At least Titus had sacrificed himself for a cause of sorts—except that he hadn't, apparently, made the ultimate sacrifice, and had even fluffed his line in Scott's edited script, and the cause had turned out to be just as futile as . . .

Tom was about to think "ours," but he knew that if Judgment was just round the corner, he wasn't entitled to that sort of lie. It was *theirs*: their sacrifice, the poor sods, to the heroism of which he had no possible claim.

Am I any better off than he is, Tom wondered. *Am I really sure that I'm alive?*

That was self-indulgence, though, and he knew it. He was alive, all right. Alive, anyway.

Absent-mindedly, Tom poured them both another glass of brandy, and filled the tea-cups, adding a dash of milk fresh from the udder that morning, but no sugar. Sugar had been in short supply for a long time

Oates stopped massaging his calves in order to take another gulp of the brandy. Even though his frostbitten face was so terrible to behold, there was an unmistakable fleshiness about it, and the way he drank, polite as it was, left no doubt at all as to his solidity. He wasn't a ghost. He wasn't a hallucination. That was a pity, on both accounts, Tom thought. Like any aristocratic manor whose foundations dated back at least to Tudor times, the house must have played host to its fair share of tragedies, rapes and murders, but there wasn't a single old soldier, crying child or white lady who walked the corridors at night, plaintively demanding succor or justice. Tom, a more imaginative child than either of his brothers, had always thought that the poor old heap had been a trifle deprived in that respect. As for hallucination . . . well, how sweet it would have been to look back and think that some of the worst things he'd seen might only have been hallucinations, and that he might simply be "doolally tap."

But Oates was real. Dead or not, he was real. Whatever he had come to ask of Tom, however absurd or horrible it turned out to be, was real too—and so was the obligation that Tom had to help him remain real. It was more than just the ties formed at school and in the army, however binding they might be; it was something more powerful than that.

"Seeds," Tom said, as if the word had somehow become the strangest in the language. "Fair enough, Titus—let's have a look."

III

OATES picked up his kitbag, reached inside, and took out a package. It was made with seemingly-ordinary brown paper, completed with string and sealing-wax—almost insultingly common-place. He put the package on the desk without rising to his feet, and resumed massaging his calves, but with an expression on his face that might have been relief, as if the act of opening the kit-bag and handing over the parcel had produced a decrease in his discomfort.

Tom cut the string with his pen-knife and un-wrapped the paper, carefully. Inside the brown paper there was a layer of cloth, which might or might not have been linen. When that was unwrapped, there was a layer of something else, to which Tom couldn't put a name: something greasy and soft. When that was un-wrapped in its turn, the "seeds" appeared.

"Seeds" was not the appellation that would have occurred to Tom, an experienced botanist, but Oates relevant vocabulary was evidently limited, and even Tom had no immediately-available substitute. The objects did not resemble beans or tubers more closely than they resembled soft-shelled eggs or insect pupae, but none of those appellations seemed entirely fitting.

There were seven of them, each as big as a child's fist and just as knobbly, not rock-hard without being sponge-squishy. They were slightly slick to the touch, seemingly more oily than damp, although nothing came off on Tom's fingers when he palpated them gently. The tegument was not reminiscent of a mollusk-shell, and he decided that the nearest earthly analogue, purely in terms of superficial appearances, might be some exotic form of pupa, belonging to a gigantic bluebottle or a gargantuan silk-moth. But he did not want to restrict his thought unduly by imposing such a fake label. There was no ready word in the language of earthly biology to describe them. They were not namable, except by awkward improvisation, so why not think of them as "seeds"?—not in the sense of making an assumption that they were plants, but in the sense that they were something designed to become something else, something full of potential to develop into something different.

Tom was surprised to find that they felt cold. That didn't make any sense. They'd been wrapped up in Oates' kitbag, the fabric of which seemed warmly protective. The temperature of the seeds should at least have been similar to the ambient temperature of the air in the study—but Tom remembered that Titus' handshake had also seemed unusually cold, well below ninety-eight Fahrenheit, as if poor undead Titus had a cold heart and cold blood. On the other hand, although Oates handshake had chilled Tom slightly, it hadn't threatened to give his fingers frostbite; it hadn't been literally icy.

Tom looked at Oates carefully. He seemed more comfortable now, as if he were warming up, even though there was no fire in the grate. Perhaps it was the effect of the brandy and tea that he now had inside him, or the mere fact that he had been welcomed into the household. His face looked more human, relatively speaking, and Tom had already deduced that he might be able to help it stay that way by not asking, at least for the time being, too many probing questions, the answers to which generally turned out to be somewhat paradoxical.

"What do you expect me to do with these, exactly, Titus?" Tom asked.

"You're the expert, Linny," was the unhelpful reply. "All I know is that they need to be placed in a suitable environment, incubated in a . . . nutritive matrix . . .

"You mean soil?"

"Soil?" Oates did not seem certain. "I suppose I do. Yes, soil . . . they need to be covered up, to begin with, snugly . . . not just nested but . . . surrounded. I don't know what the right matrix is, except that it needs blood in it . . . to be saturated."

"Ox-blood?" Tom suggested. "More appropriate than sheep, if we're breeding minotaurs?"

Oates didn't laugh at the attempted joke. "Yes," he said, "ox-blood might be best."

"Given that the minotaur of Crete was a product of biological artifice," Tom reminded his friend, "created by Daedalus, the designer of the labyrinth and thus the first great biological engineer. I had a little speech about that at Eton, remember? . . . one of my little flights of fancy."

Oates nodded. "Yes, I remember it," he said.

"Did you remember it when you used the words 'labyrinth' and 'minotaur' as nicknames for things, you . . . dreamed?"

"I don't know," Oates said, frowning as he made an effort to remember.

"It doesn't matter," Tom assured him. "We'll find out what they are, in time." In the meantime, he thought: *Vampiric seeds that need to be buried in a blood-soaked matrix. But that's not so unusual, nowadays. There are whole swathes of France and Belgium that have been abundantly fertilized by blood these last few years—particularly good for poppies, it's said, and thus, perhaps, for making laudanum. If these things were to produce a finer poppy, and a better laudanum, that wouldn't be a bad thing . . . but I can't quite believe it, odd though that is, considering the things that I do seem to be able to believe just now.*

"So what I'm supposed to do," he said, by way of summation, "is stick them in various mixtures of mineral-enriched bloody soil and hope to find one that suits them? There are only seven, though—that's not nearly enough for any kind of disciplined experimentation with different environmental regimes. If I slice one up with a microtome to examine its cellular structure under a microscope, as I'll have to do in order to find out more about it, I'll be fourteen per cent down in my sample. But at least that will allow me to attempt to produce a series of tissues-cultures, which will permit vegetative growth, if these things really are vegetable... and I ought to do that, in order to make some progress toward understanding."

"Do what you have to do, Linny," Oates said. "You don't have to grow all seven to maturity. The more the better, but the important thing is for some of them to be ready. Even one might be enough, although more would obviously be better. Nobody expects miracles."

Tom assumed that he meant that even *they* didn't expect miracles, but *they* were apparently indescribable, except by means of an improvised nickname, which presumably served the usual function of diminution, the function of making the ominous seem less ominous. Oates hasn't been in the War, when such minimizing efforts were commonplace among the enlisted men, but he had been to Eton, where they were a supposedly aristocratic affectation.

Tom knew that he was going to have to find out more about *them*, if only because it might make it a lot easier to find a way of develop the "seeds" if he could discover or deduce something about their natural life-cycle and their native ecological context. In any case, as a true scientist, he couldn't simply try to enable the seeds to develop without making every attempt to analyze their alien nature while he was doing it.

He knew full well that there were many "true scientists" who would have considered him "merely" a botanist, only a cut above a humble gardener, but for him, there was nothing mere about the science of botany. Even though Joseph Banks' contemporaries had elected him as president of the Royal Society, precious few of them had understood the true importance of the plant specimens he had collected, studied and transplanted, and as for the idiot mutineers who had completely failed to understand why the *Bounty* was transporting breadfruit, they were beyond contempt. For those reasons, as well as the binding obligations he had to Oates, Tom felt that he *had* to make every effort to understand what the mysterious entities were . . . to the extent that human understanding might be possible.

"Do you remember those blacks in the north, back in '08," Tom asked his friend, "who told us tales of jungles where there were vampire flowers that drank the blood of humans? Not that they'd ever seen a jungle, mind—we'd seen more jungle than they had—but they had their fingers firmly on the pulse of local folklore. It's a common notion in the kind of adventure stories you find in boys' books. Are these the seeds of those vampire flowers, do you think?" He didn't imagine for a moment that it could be true, but he wanted to test the direction and scope of Oates' imagination.

"No," said Oates, bluntly. "They're from much further away than any earthly jungle. I don't know what they'll produce, but I don't think we ought to worry about roses with narcotic scent and bloodthirsty petals, or carnivorous trees whose branches resemble clawed arms or snakes with avid fangs, or octopoid tentacles . . ."

He stopped suddenly, as if the idea of tentacles had rung a bell—as if, once again, his train of thought had collided with a mental bumper. After a pause, though, he resumed: "Anyway, I don't think that's the kind of danger they'll pose, if you succeed in growing them to maturity."

"But they will pose *some* kind of danger?" Tom queried.

"They might," Oates said, flatly.

"I have a wife and child," Tom said. "Not to mention three laboratory assistants, four ground staff and eight domestic servants—a whole colony to support and sustain, in effect. How *much* danger?"

"I don't know," Oates repeated, bluntly.

If Oates had said that he wished that he did know, Tom wouldn't have believed him. Instead, he only added: "I'm sorry, Linny." Tom wasn't entirely sure that he believed that, either.

Tom considered saying no, but only for form's sake, having already run through an adequate number of reasons why he couldn't possibly refuse his friend's request. If he said no he would miss out on an unprecedented experiment. He would miss out on a mystery. He would also miss out on the danger, but if he had chanced to find one of those vampire plants of legend in Africa, he would have gone to any lengths to get their seeds back to a controlled environment, where he could grow and nurture them, study and marvel at them . . . even feed them, if he had to, irrespective of any danger they might pose. The entities that Oates was offering him were real and tangible. What did it matter that they needed blood to constitute an adequate "nutritive matrix"? They were from another world. Maybe not from another planet, but from somewhere or somewhen exceedingly strange. How could he even think of saying no?

"It's all right, Titus," he said. "I'll be glad to help. I can't promise you anything, but I'll do my very best, for you and the barrel-boys, whoever they are."

Oates tried to smile. His face wasn't really equipped for it, for the moment, but the armchair, the brandy and the tea seemed to be doing him good. He seemed to be adapting well to the environment, soaking up its comfort and its atmosphere: its *homeliness*. He was collecting himself, Tom thought, becoming more Oatesy than ... but he didn't have a name to put to *that*. Oates now gave the impression of being more alive than dead, at any rate.

Oates, Tom recalled to mind, with a conscious effort, was a genuine hero: a man who had at least tried to lose his life while making a Quixotic gesture, after trying to go where no man had gone before, and only failing because Amundsen had got their first, having started with better equipment, a better plan and without Robert Scott's delusions of grandeur. Oates had walked out of Scott's tent into a whiteout, and fallen ... where? In time, if the seeds could be planted, and if they could germinate and grow, Tom thought that he had every chance of finding the answer to that challenging question—and he needed that. He needed a problem, with the possibility of a solution, in order to help him recover a sense of purpose in life. And Titus had come back from the dead to give me that opportunity, even if he hadn't quite made it *all the way back*, as yet. Tom owed it to him to do everything he could, not just because he was his oldest friend and there had been too many friends—brothers, even—for whom he hadn't been able to do anything at all, but because he was a godsend. If any one of his other old friends had come back, dead or otherwise, to ask him for a favor, however absurd or dangerous, he would have been glad to do it, if he had still been capable of gladness. He would have been *determined* to do it, even desperate. What was a little danger in that circumstance? As long as Helen could be kept out of it, and the brat.

Tom squinted at his visitor, trying to make out his familiar features more clearly—or, at least, trying to figure out why he still couldn't quite do that, even though he knew that it had to be Lawrence Oates: good old Titus.

"But what if I fail?" he said.

"Don't worry about that, Linny," said Oates. "Just try. That's all any of us can do. Nobody expects any more from you than that."

Again, Oates had emptied his glass and his cup. Tom looked yet again at his lower legs, which seemed to be swollen inside their ill-fitting boots. He was trying, judiciously, to think of the right way to rephrase his oft-repeated request to take a look at Oates's feet, when the door to the study opened and the brat came in. She was forbidden to do that, of course, but she rarely took any notice of prohibitions—which was why Tom often thought of her as "the brat" even though she was the apple of his eye. When he had been her age, he would have been very wary indeed of doing anything that his own father, let alone, the Old Earl, had forbidden him to do, but times had changed, and Mercy knew full well that there was no danger of corporal punishment for the sin of disobedience.

Evidently, she hadn't realized that her father had a visitor. She didn't know that she was interrupting, so she had simply burst in, taking it for granted that Tom would be as pleased to see her as he could be, even if he was busy—as he always was—and would put on a pretence of sorts even if he couldn't manage to be pleased.

Whatever it was she had intended to say died on her lips. She came to an abrupt halt, and stared. Children could do that, Tom knew. The poor mite wasn't old enough to understand "conduct unbecoming." She was too busy just becoming.

Oates looked better than he had when he had paused on the driveway, but he still looked bad—not quite as dead, but still possessed of a face that even a mother would have had difficulty loving.

Tom thought that it would be best to act as if everything were normal. What alternative was there, in any case?

"This is my daughter Mary, Titus," Tom told Oates. "We call her Mercy. She's seven. Mercy, this is an old friend of mine from the army, Captain Oates."

"Were you hurt in the war?" Mercy asked the dead man, mildly.

Tom realized that the mildness wasn't feigned. Mercy honestly and truly wasn't frightened, or even shocked—much less so than he had been, at any rate. The name didn't mean anything to her, so she had no idea that "Captain Oates" had been famously declared dead shortly before she was born. As for the face ... she had seen worse.

In the latter days of the war Helen, under the compulsion to *do her bit*, had allowed the east wing of the house to be turned into a military sanitarium for men who'd been badly hit by the shrapnel of shell-fire, in more ways than one. Mercy had already seen too many things that popular wisdom considered it unwise for a child her age to see, and she had proved popular wisdom wrong. She had earned her nickname. She had seen men who had been burned and men who had been blasted. She had played ball with some of them on the front lawn. She had no real notion of the possible range of human injury, but she knew that it was possible to be horribly disfigured, and that it happened to many young men who were reckoned to be heroes. She simply didn't know that what had become of Oates' face was any more improbable or disgusting than what had become of others she'd seen.

"I was shot in the leg in Africa," Oates told her, deliberately misunderstanding the question. "One of my legs is shorter than the other now." The answer had the effect, at least, of directing Mercy's stare away from Oates' face. She looked at his legs, but he was sitting down; she hadn't seen him limping. The answer sufficed, however. Mercy was used to not getting straight answers. She nodded, sympathetically.

"Welcome to Andersley, Captain," she said, politely. "Will you be staying long?"

Slightly discomfited, Oates didn't reply.

"Yes," said Tom, "Captain Oates will be staying with us for a while. We have some work to do in the tropical house."

"That's nice," said Mercy—and Tom could see that she meant it. She really thought that it would be pleasant to have a visitor. Perhaps she thought that Oates would play ball with her on the lawn. That was probably something that she thought badly wounded and shell-shocked soldiers routinely did, when they had someone to play with . . . someone not too big and not too clever, who could match their own incapacity. But she was also being kind; Tom was proud of her.

Tom was also glad, to the extent that he was capable of gladness, that Oates' being here was all right . . . with Mercy, at least. That removed one potential problem, although he had not previously given it any thought. The other, the presence and awkwardness of which he had not considered, suddenly loomed large in his consciousness. What on earth was he going to tell Helen?

He had no time to think about it, or to formulate any kind of plan; it was far too late for that.

Helen came in at that point, chasing after Mercy but a long way behind, as usual.

"Sorry, Tom," she said, automatically. Then she stopped dead, having only taken one step away from the open doorway.

For a moment, she almost let her astonishment show, because she did know the difference between a war wound and whatever was afflicting Titus, but she was made of exceedingly stern stuff now. She wasn't the same wife that she had been before Tom went away to war. She was familiar now with the horrible, the inexpressible and the paradoxical, and that familiarity had not ended with the armistice. She was doubtless horrified, but she controlled her reflexive reaction. She barely glanced at Tom before turning her attention to Mercy, protectively. She knew how she had to conduct herself, and there was no awkward shifting of mental gears as she added: "I didn't know you had company, Tom."

Oates had stood up, hoisted to his feet by an ancient reflex, an instinctive politeness that had survived even the Mountains of Madness and beyond. He bowed politely, a trifle lop-sidedly.

Tom made a superhuman effort to keep his voice level as he said: "This is my wife, Helen, Titus. Helen, this is Captain Oates. You've heard me mention him many a time; I knew him at school, and in Africa, latterly in the dragoons."

Unlike Mercy, Helen knew perfectly well who Captain Oates was, and not just because Tom had, indeed, mentioned him many a time as a companion at Eton and in the army. She knew perfectly well that he was supposed to be dead, but she was a Yorkshirewoman, well-bred and well-educated. She responded to Oates' bow with a polite inclination of the head and said: "I do apologize, Captain Oates. I had no forewarning of your visit, and it has taken me somewhat by surprise. Tom is a trifle . . . forgetful with regard to domestic matters. Will you be staying for dinner?"

"Yes, he will," Tom interjected, swiftly. "I've invited him for an indefinite stay. We'll be doing some work together. I'm sorry that I couldn't give you more notice, but Captain Oates' arrival was a surprise to me too."

"I'm very sorry, Lady Andersley," Oates said, smoothly. "I would have given you and Tom advance warning had I been able to do so, but circumstances did not permit it. I'm truly sorry to have alarmed you. I realize that you must have heard reports of my death, but I'm not a ghost."

Tom tried to read Helen's expression, but her mask of politeness was rigid. He did not suppose for an instant that Helen really believed that the hideous scarecrow in front of her was Lawrence Oates, and he strongly suspected that she must assume that, after teetering on the brink for a long time, her husband had finally gone completely mad.

"I'd better go and tell Janet that there'll be an extra setting for dinner," Helen said, only a trifle uncertainly. Her voice implied that it wasn't the only thing she'd have to warn the staff about. She put a protective arm around Mercy's shoulder, although Mercy was not giving the slightest sign of wanting protection, but she didn't leave the room immediately. Instead, she waited, presumably to see whether anyone was going to volunteer some kind of explanation. Had Tom had one to offer he would have been only too pleased, but all he could think of to say, for the moment, was: "Captain Oates is my oldest friend, as you know, Helen. I hope that you'll make him welcome here."

"Of course, Tom," she said, apparently deciding that the best thing to do was to maintain what she assumed to be a charade, for Mercy's sake. "You know that any friend of yours is welcome here, Captain Oates more than anyone."

Tom felt as proud of his wife as he was of his daughter. He already was—he had an idea of how difficult it had been for her to *do her bit*, helping to look after the walking wounded and the walking dead, including wounded men who would never walk again, or have faces that would not test a mother's love to destruction—but the present situation was so far beyond the normal call of duty that he marveled at her composure . . . without, of course, giving any external evidence of his marveling.

"In fact, Helen," Tom continued, "I need to have a look at Captain Oates' feet. He was having trouble walking when he arrived. It would be an enormous help if you could ask Janet to send me a bowl of warm water, some carbolic soap and some bandages." He was not sure himself whether he was simply offering her an excuse to leave the room, or whether he was trying to expel her because her presence was discomfiting.

Either way, it didn't work.

"If there's a serious problem," she replied, sternly, "you should have summoned me immediately. I'll have a look myself—it's become my area of expertise, after all." That was not the answer that Tom had been fishing for, but he had no time to be disconcerted, because she immediately turned to Oates and said: "You must forgive my husband, Captain Oates; in spite of his experiences in France he has no proper sense of urgency in these matters. He should have sent for me instantly, instead of sitting here drinking brandy and ordering pots of tea. Tom, will *you* go ask Janet to bring the things you listed, while I assess the problem properly. Take Mercy with you, please."

Tom hesitated, wondering whether he ought to exert his supposed authority in order to regain the lost ground, but he judged that it would be a bad idea. He nodded meekly, and took Mercy by the hand.

When they were in the corridor, on the way to the servants' parlor, Mercy said: "Mummy's upset with you. Have you done something wrong?"

"Yes," Tom said, "but I couldn't help it."

"She'll forgive you," Mercy opined. "She always does."

That stung. "I'm sorry that she has to," he murmured.

"You don't have to be," the child assured him. "She knows that you're ill. A lot of the men who stayed here were ill that way, as well as being hit by bullets or burned I played ball with them, if they could. I think it helped them. Some of them got better."

The last remark was perfectly innocent; Mercy was not employing it, as an adult might have done, to signify that some of them had not, or even to compliment herself on having done her bit. Even so, there was a veiled criticism within the innocence, whose subtlety did credit to a seven-year-old, in Tom's opinion. Mercy was suggesting that if he would only play ball with her a little more, instead of spending his time shut up one or other of the greenhouses, he might be "getting better" a little more rapidly.

Tom thought that she might be right; instead of making any promises that he might not be able to keep, however, he said: "Captain Oates will be working with me in the greenhouses, I'm afraid. He won't be able to play ball with you."

If Mercy was disappointed by that reply, she didn't show it. Even at seven, she was modeling herself on her mother. Tom wondered whether her lack of reaction was evidence that she was so used to disappointment that she had become inured to it.

He handed his daughter over to Beth, one of the parlor-maids, who seemed to be at a loose end, and went to relay the commission to Janet, who merely arched an eyebrow in surprise when he appeared in the kitchen.

"We have a visitor, Janet," he said. "Can you please ask Maggie to fill a bowl with hot water, and assemble some carbolic and bandages so that I can take them to Lady Andersley in the study, and please have the bed in the best guest-room made up and a bath run. There'll be an extra place-setting for dinner tonight, and every evening until further notice."

"Yes, sir," said Janet tersely. Technically, she ought to have addressed Tom as "milord," but she had lived most of her own life under the old regime, and still thought of Tom, even at nearly forty years of age, as the baby of the family. She would have addressed Jack as "milord," had he lived to inherit the title, but he hadn't.

As soon as he had collected the relevant materials from the kitchen-maid, Tom returned to the study. Oates had removed his boots and socks at last. His feet were badly discolored, the discoloration varying from blue-gray to black, and the hardened skin was cracked and peeling."

"Tom!" said Helen, angrily. "How could you let the captain sit here in this condition? He must have been in agony."

"Actually, no," Oates put in. "It was uncomfortable while I was on my feet, but once I had sat down, they barely itched. Please don't blame Linny—it's entirely my own fault. He asked me several times to take my boots off, but I didn't. I needed time to collect myself. I'm sorry."

The move deflected the anger away from Tom without bringing it down on himself. Nevertheless, Helen's voice was severe as she said: "That's frostbite, and a bad case. Your face and fingers are frostbitten too, but I think that will heal, given time. I'm really not so sure about your feet; there's a strong chance that you might lose a few toes."

A few toes! Tom thought. *She can say that as if it were something trivial, something run-of-the-mill. She's no longer capable of horror. Even here, in this utmost backwater of civilization, she was in the war . . . with an absent husband and a little child. Poor girl!*

But as he looked down at his wife, on her knees, he could see all too plainly that she was no longer a girl. She had been eighteen when he married her, whereas he had been thirty-two, but the age-gap seemed to have narrowed considerably in the strange interim. She was no longer the same woman that she had been before, but she had more excuse for that than he had for not being the same man.

"It's not as bad as it has been," Oates said, calmly. "Before I left the hut, I think, there was a touch of gangrene, but that seems to have cleared up, and even the frostbite has begun to heal. All it needs is time."

"Gangrene doesn't *clear up*," Helen stated, flatly. She knew that; she had seen gangrenous limbs.

"Nor does death, normally," Oates observed, mildly, "but I think you'll agree, Lady Andersley, that for a dead man, I'm not doing too badly. By comparison, a little vanished gangrene is surely a minor matter,"

Helen's head was bowed, as she was dabbing Oates' swollen feet with a sponge and cleaning them with carbolic soap, and Tom could only see the back of her head, so he could not measure her reaction to that speech. Oates did not wince as the carbolic soap met his discolored and deformed soles.

After a short pause, Helen looked over her shoulder at her husband. "This isn't a joke, is it, Tom? You really believe that this man is *the* Captain Oates?"

"It is," said Tom. "There's no doubt about it. Not many people would recognize him, I suppose, but I can't be mistaken. It's Titus. Impossible as it seems, you have to believe me."

Helen looked up at Oates then, staring at his damaged face. She had seen photographs of Oates, but she wasn't trying to recognize the man in the photographs in the man before her. She was searching his bloated features for some evidence of deceit, or insanity.

"I'm truly sorry, Lady Andersley," said Oates. "I don't understand it any more than you do, but Linny's absolutely right. Anyone else could be mistaken, but not him. Believe me, I have my own doubts. If anyone else had said to me: 'Yes, I recognize you; you're Lawrence Oates,' I would have doubted them and doubted myself; but Linny I trust, even though it's nearly ten years since we last shook hands. If he says that I'm who I think I am, no matter how impossible that seems, I believe him. It's not necessary that you should, and I won't make any strenuous effort to convince you—think of me as Captain X, if you wish, or merely as Mister X—but please humor my . . . delusion, and Tom's. I need him to believe me."

Had she been a southerner, Tom thought, Helen would probably have sent for a couple of doctors to have him certified as insane, but she was a Yorkshirewoman, hand-picked by the real Earl of Andersley, his grandfather. That, even more than the fact that she had spent more than two years running a convalescent home for badly injured serviceman, meant that there was no question of her trying to ship him off to an asylum. She would play the game, by the rules she had been taught—and the servants would play it too, on her instructions, because they would take the view that they didn't have to understand, but merely had to follow orders, whether those who gave the orders were sane or not.

"If Tom says that you're Captain Oates," Helen said, soberly, "that's good enough for me."

Tom knew that she meant it, even though he had done nothing, not merely in the last few months but in all the years of their marriage, to warrant that kind of faith, or that kind of loyalty.

"Thank you, Lady Andersley," said Oates. "Linny is a very lucky man." He said it with a perfectly straight face; it wasn't a joke. He added: "If and when we have an explanation, we'll share it with you, but for the moment, we're as mystified as you are."

Helen pursed her lips. She still had Oates' left foot in her hand. She knew that he was perfectly real, a creature of human flesh, albeit slightly, and perhaps temporarily, spoiled. She knew, too, having seen and felt that foot and its counterpart, that he really had been somewhere very cold, apparently quite recently.

"The feet will get better," Tom told her, weakly. "All they need is time."

"They're already better than they were," Oates added. "It's very kind of your husband to have welcomed me with such equanimity, and I believe that he's right to be optimistic about my condition. Given time and a little help, I believe that I'll make a full recovery."

Tom was surprised by the fact that Oates really did seem manifestly better now than he had done before the door opened to admit Mercy, and he was sure that it wasn't an effect of hot water and carbolic soap. Oates was reacting to the environment, and to Mercy and Helen. Their mere appearance had helped him to get a firmer grip on himself. Once again, the impossible man tried to smile, and almost succeeded.

"I'm delighted to hear you say so, Captain Oates," Helen said, "although I must admit that I can't quite share your confidence. Whatever we can do to assist your recovery, though, we'll be only too pleased to do."

"You're very kind," said Oates. "As kind as you're beautiful, in fact. As I said, Linny's a very lucky man."

"Why do you call him *Linny?*" Helen queried, curiously.

"I'm sorry," said Oates. "It's an old nickname, which no one else can have used for years. I meant to say *Tom.*"

"I never heard it before," said Helen. "But then, I didn't have a chance to meet you during our courtship and the early days of our marriage. It's a pity that you couldn't make it to our wedding—but hardly any of Tom's old friends from school or the army were there; it was a very quiet affair."

Tom presumed that Oates' arithmetic would easily be adequate to calculate the probable date of Helen's marriage from the fact that Mecy was seven years old, but he thought it worth taking the trouble to say: "It was back in '11; the Terra Nova expedition had already set out. As Helen says, it was a quiet affair, in the local church—only family. Grandfather didn't want a fuss. No one came up from London. I didn't want any military show, but I would have invited you, obviously, if you had been in England."

"Of course," said Oates, smoothly. "I'm sorry that I didn't have an opportunity to meet you then, Lady Andersley, but I'm delighted to have the privilege now, and I hope that it won't be any trouble. I'm terribly sorry to barge in on you unannounced, but I had to ask a favor of your husband, urgently, and I had no way of getting in touch with him."

"There's a post office in the village," Helen pointed out, mildly, "and Tom's address is the same now as it was when he was at Eton."

"Yes, course," said Oates. "I've been here before, and it's not a difficult address to remember. Really, I have no excuse for not having written, or even sent a telegram; I hope you can forgive me."

Tom remembered what Mercy had said about her mother always forgiving, but he suspected that her supply of forgiveness must be running very low by now

Helen had finished winding bandages around Oates' feet, and she got to her feet. "The dressing will have to be changed in a couple of days," she said. "We'll see then whether the loss of the toes seems inevitable. In the meantime, keep the bandages out of the bathwater, if you can manage the contortion, and tread softly. I presume you'll be working with my husband in the hothouses." She was looking at the desk, where the seven "seeds" that had been removed from Oates' kitbag were still neatly laid out on their various unfolded wrappings.

"That's right," Tom said. "We have a lot of work to do, and I don't know how long it will take. We'll be working alone in the tropical house, while Alice, Sally and Maureen look after the projects in the other greenhouses."

"But we'll see you for dinner every evening, won't we?" Helen said. "And you'll spare a little time when you can for Mercy, won't you?"

"Of course," said Tom, only a trifle hollowly.

"I'll do my best not to be any trouble, Lady Andersley," Oates assured her.

"It's no trouble at all, I assure you, Captain Oates," she replied, in a honeyed tone, carefully refusing to reveal any consciousness on her part that the Day of Judgment must be close at hand, since the Resurrection had evidently begun. "I hope that we can assist you in your recovery."

Silently, Tom thanked her for that *we*. She was, he thought, a genuine hero.

"We've had other men here with hurt faces," Mercy put in, helpfully, from the doorway, evidently having given Beth the slip, as she was inclined to do even when her curiosity was not as sorely piqued, simply for the pleasure of exercising her right of disobedience. "We did our bit. I played with them. An American taught me baseball. I'm a good pitcher, but the bat was too heavy for me, and his mitt was too big. I did my best anyway, and he gave me his baseball when he went home. I'll pitch it for you, if you like . . . I know there was no baseball at Eton, but I've offered to teach Daddy. I can teach you instead."

"You're very kind, Mary," Oates told her, "but it will have to wait until my feet are better, I fear. Please forgive me."

"There's nothing to forgive," Mercy said, echoing a phrase that she had heard her mother employ many a time, but pronouncing it with more conviction. Her sincerity was not feigned, even though there was, in fact, a great deal to forgive. Mercy had not yet learned to make such judgments accurately

IV

HELEN wasn't so painstakingly polite, of course, once dinner was over and Oates had retired diplomatically to his room, excusing himself by pleading exceptional tiredness.

During dinner, the conversation had been conspicuously stilted, and not just because of the presence of Janet and Linda, filling in for the butler and footman who had both left the house during the War, never to return or be replaced. Oates excused his retirement with the utmost politeness, and Tom had no difficulty believing that he really was exceptionally tired, because the evidence was so clear. He went up to the guest room with him, to make sure that Oates had everything he needed, but only stayed for a couple of minutes before coming back down and retreating immediately to the study. He almost locked the door, but felt that that would be taking cowardice a step too far, and he feared that Helen might finally lose her temper if he tried to send her away.

He had hardly sat down at the desk and bowed his head in order to pore over the seeds before the door opened again.

"Well," his wife said, unceremoniously, "I thought I'd seen everything, but I was wrong, wasn't I? Not even almost everything, it seems."

"I could have looked after Titus' feet myself," Tom said, uneasily, "or you could have asked Linda to do it. You didn't have to do it yourself."

"Didn't I?" she retorted. "You weren't so keen to look after people's feet when you first came back, before the last of the casualties was finally shipped out. It was definitely my job then, lady of the manor or not. Evidently, my days of playing Florence Nightingale aren't over yet. Not that I mind that, particularly, but . . . Captain Oates?" Her voice was incredulous, but it seemed to Tom that there was a certain artificiality about the incredulity. "*The* Captain Oates? What on earth are you playing at, Tom?"

"It was a surprise to me too," Tom said, defensively. "Perhaps even more than it was to you. You never knew him. The servants seem to have taken it in their stride, including the instruction to maintain his incognito . . . but Janet is the only one who actually met Titus, before we went to Africa. To the younger ones, he's just a name, one more reported death among thousands, and it's not the first such report that turned to be . . . exaggerated."

"*Exaggerated?*" Helen repeated. "He wasn't simply recorded in dispatches as missing in action. The man disappeared *in Antarctica*, seven years ago. He can't possibly be alive. That would be beyond miraculous."

"But he is alive," Tom was content to state. "You've touched his feet. It's not exactly Saint Thomas putting his hand in the wound in Jesus' side, but it's near enough. He's alive. He can't be, but he is."

"Saint Thomas met Jesus after an absence of a few days," Helen said. "Oates has been . . . gone for seven years. Where? How?"

"I don't know," Tom told her. "He's unclear about it himself, but he's already making some progress remembering. He just needs time, and careful handling. By me, I hasten to add. You don't have to do anything, honestly. I'll take care of everything, I promise."

"You really are an infuriating man," she retorted. "I ought to slap your face. Don't pretend to be doing me a favor, when you're thinking entirely of yourself . . . not that you've been capable of doing anything else these last few months. Evidently, you don't give a hoot about me any longer, if you ever did, but damn it, Tom, you have to make an effort for Mercy's sake. You have to."

Tom was hurt by the accusation that he might never have "given a hoot." The marriage might have been arranged, as all family marriages had been in the days of the real Lord Andersley, but he had not only done his best to love his wife but had succeeded—far better than Jack and Hal. When Jack's Lilian had died giving birth to what would have been the heir that he had been expected to produce, Jack had hardly been able to shed a tear even for the stillborn boy. As for Hal, his Josephine had died in India, so Tom had no idea whether she had been mourned there, or to what extent, but she had been, in his grandfather's terminology, "barren," and thus had failed in her duty, so she had not been mourned unduly at Andersley. Lord Andersley would doubtless have "fixed up" his widowed sons again had the War not intervened, but any plans he might have formed for them had been torpedoed like a hapless troop-ship in the Channel as soon as war had been declared.

What would the Old Earl have thought of the present Earl, had he lived? Tom wondered. He would probably have forgiven him for siring a daughter, because that was simply the luck of the draw, but not for having failed to follow up forthwith with a son. "There's plenty of time, Thomas," he would have said, had he still been alive. "Just buckle down and get on with the job." And he would have been right about the plenitude of the time; Helen was in her twenties, still perfectly fertile, so far as anyone could tell. But . . .

"I'm sorry," he said. "I know I ought to make more effort. It's not that I don't want to."

"That's what I keep telling myself, and Mercy too—but it's becoming hard to believe. And this . . . it's the last straw, Tom. You cannot possibly believe that that man is the Captain Oates who died on the Scott expedition."

"In fact," Tom said, stubbornly, "I can't believe that he isn't—but it doesn't matter. Believe what you like. The point is that he and I have a job to do. He brought me these." He waved his hand over the objects on the desk, appealing to her curiosity as a means of changing the subject.

"What are they?" she demanded, taking the bait.

"He calls them seeds," Tom said. "Perhaps they are, although they're like no seeds I've ever seen before."

"Seeds from the Antarctic?" Her voice was incredulous, but again there was a certain hesitation in her incredulity.

"Possibly—but not from the Antarctic as it is today. If that's where they originated, they must have been lying dormant under the ice for a very long time. But when Titus jumped into the crevasse, he didn't just land at the bottom of a pit. Like Alice in the rabbit-hole, he ended up in some kind of wonderland, displaced in time, space or some other dimension."

Helen's gaze went to the bookshelves, where there were all manner of esoteric texts, which she was too polite to refer to by any adjective more insulting than "strange," as well as a copy of the complete works of Lewis Carroll and a respectable array of textbooks of botany,

"And he wants you to plant them, in the big greenhouse?" she queried.

"That's right."

"To grow what?"

"I don't know, and I don't think he does either. It will be . . . a voyage of discovery. If I succeed, that is. I might not."

Helen picked up one of the "seeds," weighed it in her hand, turned it over and over, and set it down again. "It's cold," she observed.

"Yes, it is," Tom agreed; he did not venture any hypothesis that might explain the fact.

"Well," she said, eventually, "I don't suppose it's that much more bizarre than what you've been doing the last few months. Bananas, in England! And breadfruit! Not to mention pineapples."

"You'll hardly know the difference," Tom told her.

"If you think that's reassuring," she told him, "it isn't. Adding Captain Oates to the mix just serves to emphasize the fact that it was ... uncomfortable before. I suppose I'd better leave you to it, then. I don't suppose you'll be knocking on my door when you come up?"

Tom and Helen had always had separate bedrooms, because that had been the way things had been done in the house, in Victorian times. Helen had not approved, in the beginning, but while the Old Earl was still alive, no one's disapproval but his had ever counted for anything. When Tom had returned home after the War, she had made the suggestion that perhaps they ought to adopt new rules, but he had evaded the issue. He had not "knocked on her door" since, not because he didn't want to, but because he didn't want to write any metaphorical checks that he felt certain that his body couldn't cash. He made no reply to her discreet provocation, and Helen withdrew.

Tom breathed out and delved in his desk drawer for a large magnifying glass. He examined the tegument of one of the seeds with minute care, and then examined another, which seemed to be similar in all respects. *Like a hard, dried plum*, he thought, *or the cupule of an exotic chestnut, or perhaps simply the pericarpus—if it is part of a plant rather than an animal egg or pupa. Time will tell.*

He was tempted to start a dissection right away, but thought it best to wait until morning, when Oates could observe. He would have to dissect one, in order to study its internal anatomy and learn what he could from its structure, but only one. The other six, he would attempt to grow.

He knew that he would have to dissect Oates too, metaphorically, and make what attempt he could to learn what he could from an analysis of his speech—not that it would probably make any more sense, rationally, than the observations he had been able to make of his frostbite, which was clearly paradoxical, partly healed but seemingly recent—certainly not seven years old. It made no sense. Perhaps mercifully, Tom thought, he had been a stranger to things that made sense for quite a while. He could take irrationality in his stride, and although he had been fortunate enough to avoid literal frostbite in the trenches, while some of the men under his command hadn't been as lucky, he didn't feel that he had avoided a certain metaphorical frostbite, which wasn't as disgusting to the eye as Oates' but often gave him twinges when people said the wrong thing, or even looked at him in certain ways.

Helen had tried to cleanse and bandage that wound too, but in much the same way that the dressings she'd applied to Oates' feet were tokenistic rather than capable of any real effect, her measures hadn't manifested any real healing power. That had disappointed both of them, because they both felt that it ought to have worked.

He was still peering impotently at the seeds when Janet knocked on the study door to enquire whether he needed anything before she too retired for the night.

Nothing that you can supply, he thought—but all he said was: "Thank you Janet, but no."

Atypically, she didn't simply retire. "Is that really the same Lieutenant Oates who visited the house as a young man?" she asked, hesitantly.

"One and the same," Tom confirmed, "insofar as any of us is the same, any more. But he's a captain now, just as I was by the time the War ended."

"He didn't die in the Antarctic?" she said.

"If he did," Tom said, content to state the obvious, "he's come back from the dead."

"Why?"

That was typical of Janet; the impossible she could believe, or pretend to—but she still wanted to know why.

Tom elected deliberately to misunderstand the question. "He wants me to grow some seeds for him."

Janet wasn't content with the evasion. She was an officer of sorts within the house, and she didn't feel that her role was simply to do, and leave understanding to those who claimed that they could. She too was a hero of sorts, a housekeeper who had obtained a field promotion to substitute the butler, because butlers were in such desperately short supply. She could be content not to understand, if no understanding was possible, but she felt obliged to enquire. At the very least, Tom had to convince her that no understanding was possible.

"Why?" she asked again, employing her entitlement as a Yorkshirewoman to be blunt, with an aristocratic master she had known since he was a babe in arms.

"Apparently," Tom went on, "he suggested to someone that I might be able to do it—talked me up a bit, I suspect. I suspect that was the only way he could obtain permission to come back here for any length of time. I don't think he's really convinced that I can do it, but hinting that I might be able to succeed was the only way he could get a furlough from . . . wherever. I don't really understand, and it seems to hurt him when I ask, but I hope that, in time . . . well, we'll see."

"Lady Andersley doesn't believe that he's who he says he is," the housekeeper said, flatly. She could read Helen like a book.

"I know," Tom said, "but she's willing to humor us. The War has made quite a lot of us doubt that we were who we thought we had been. Contradiction only makes things worse. Helen knows that. Can I rely on you to support us, Janet?"

"Certainly, sir," she said.

"And to stop the servants gossiping?"

"That's impossible, I fear, sir, but I try to keep order as best I can. I don't have the authority that Hollis used to have, but I do my best."

"I know you do, Janet," Tom said, "And I'm immensely grateful to you. You're the rock on which Andersley stands; without you, it would collapse."

The housekeeper blushed slightly, although she must think, privately, that the praise was only her due.

Tom tried to remember the last time that he had been amazed by the impossible, when it happened in front of him, but he couldn't. Africa had desensitized him even before he had been recommissioned in '14. Now he had brought that desensitization home . . . but there was a sense in which he had brought everything home, because he hadn't been able to leave it behind.

Janet abandoned the Inquisition. She knew how to be patient, in confrontation with the impossible. During the War, she had been very nearly the only person left on the estate, except for Helen and the vicar, who could read fluently. Even before the east wing had been converted into a sanitarium, she had had to make distressing rounds, in order to read letters and telegrams to women who didn't understand, didn't want to understand, and prayed day and night for the impossible to come true. The women of the estate hadn't wanted the vicar, and they hadn't even wanted Helen, even though they knew that she was a wife and mother like them; they had wanted Janet, because, although she didn't have the authority that Hollis had used to have, and wasn't an angel, like Helen, she had had their intimate trust in a way that a butler or an angel couldn't. Helen had had to pretend to be an archangel, when the invalids arrived—it was a matter of adaptation to her environment—but Janet had only had to continue being Janet the housekeeper, for everyone.

"Is the captain going to be staying long?" she asked, dutifully playing the part of Janet the housekeeper.

"I hope so," said Tom. "And he needs to be made welcome. I don't know where he's been, but I'm pretty sure that he'll be better off here. He needs rest and recuperation. He didn't show me the wound in his thigh, but he confessed that it had opened again in the Antarctic because of scurvy, and the scar tissue will need time to form again. Whether his ruined toes can heal, I don't know, but if they can, that will take time too. At the very least, he needs to get used to being warm again. The cold seems to have seeped into his bones."

Janet inclined her head respectfully. "I'll see to it that he's made welcome, sir," she said. "And if his dressings need changing, there's no reason for Lady Andersley to do it. The War's over now."

"No, Janet, it isn't," Tom said, softly. "There's an armistice—a cease-fire—but that's all. The war isn't over, and I'm not sure that it ever will be. Things will never go back to the way they were in grandfather's day. We'll just have to carry on making the best of things."

Except that we're not, he carefully refrained from adding. *We're only avoiding the worst of things, and not very successfully.*

"Yes sir," said Janet. "Good night, sir."

"Good night, Janet. And thank you."

The housekeeper nodded her head politely, and closed the study door behind her.

Tom knew that that, too, was an armistice of sorts, which would stifle conflict for a while, but that it left a great many problems unsolved—first of all, the problem of Oates' injuries. He thought that he really ought to have insisted on looking at Oates' thigh, where he had been wounded thirteen years ago. If scurvy really had caused the collagen of the scar to break down and opened the wound again, it might need more expert attention than he could offer in order to avoid infection. Even the toes might require amputation, if the necrotic appearance of the tissue was as ominous as it looked. That would require a surgeon—a surgeon who was bound to ask questions to which Tom and Oates could not provide plausible answers. There was also his friend's mental condition to consider. It was all very well to assume, glibly, that it was something akin to "shell shock," but that was just jargon, a vague label that covered up the absence of a real explanation. Perhaps that needed an expert analysis too—except that Tom had not an atom of confidence in so-called alienists. And as Janet had said, there was no way to prevent the servants from gossiping, and wondering, and speculating about madness and imposture.

It doesn't matter, he thought. *We'll be in the greenhouse most of the time, or here, out of sight and out of mind. I'll put a padlock on the tropical house, and forbid entry to anyone but myself and Oates. Alice, Sally and Maureen will understand; they know that it's a controlled environment, into which people can't simply go carelessly—and anyway, they'll do as they're told.*

He knew that it would work to his advantage that the staff, with the exception of the two aged groundsmen, were all female at present; the local males who had come back from the war had found more lucrative opportunities for employment in Sheffield, Bradford or Hull than in the wolds, where even farm laborers were now in direly short supply. A generation had been lost, and would not soon be replaced. Mercifully, Alice, Maureen and Sally were perfectly capable of looking after everything in the subsidiary greenhouses; they were intelligent and efficient, and not only understood the work that he was doing with potatoes and cereals, but had the discipline to manage the experimental designs. As for the tropical house, he and Oates would be able to supervise all the fruit trees while also nurturing the mysterious "seeds," if nurturing them proved to be possible.

Tom turned up the commutator controlling the brightness of his desk lamp, picked up one of the "seeds" and held it up to the dazzling bulb, still wondering at its continued coldness; but he soon moved it away, afraid that the radiation might warm it up and that the warming might have a deleterious effect. He wrapped the seven seeds up again, carefully, and put them in a drawer.

As long as they don't produce a giant beanstalk, he thought, but then changed his mind. *Why not?* he mused. *A little giant-hunting might be fun, and I really ought to give the shotguns a little exercise. The rooks are beginning to proliferate and the derelict land around the old mines is becoming a safe haven for them. Back in the day, the farmers would have organized shoots and mounted a massacre, but they don't seem to have the same community spirit that they once had.* He knew, though, that the Jack in the fairy tale had actually been golden goose-hunting; the giant had simply got in the way. The seeds Oates had brought him might conceivably be beans of some sort, but Tom hadn't had to sell the family cow to get them, so the analogy failed at step one.

When he went upstairs to bed the house was silent. The corridors were dark, but there was a chink of light under Helen's door, and one under Mercy's. Tom hesitated, asking himself whether he ought to knock on Helen's door, but discarded the idea almost immediately. Instead, he opened Mercy's door. She was in her nightgown but out of bed, playing with her doll's house.

"You should be asleep, Mercy," he said, mildly. "Get into bed now, there's a good girl."

Obediently, Mercy climbed into bed. "Will you read me a story?" she said, hopefully.

"You can read for yourself now," Tom told her. "You don't need anyone to read to you any more. Anyway, it's far too late, and you really ought to have put your light out long ago and gone to sleep. I'm going to bed myself; I have to be up early in the morning."

"To do what?" she asked. Tom knew that it was just a stalling tactic, but he answered the question anyway.

"I have to start work on the seeds that Captain Oates brought me."

"That won't take long," Mercy opined. "You only have to bury them and leave them to grow."

"It's not that simple," Tom told her. "I'm going to slice one of them up very thinly, and use a microscope to examine the cellular structure—if it has a cellular structure. Then I'll try to start some tissue-cultures in glass dishes. I'll try to develop two of the seeds in nutrient solutions in tanks, and bury four in pots to start with, in different soil-mixtures. I'll have to observe them all carefully, at regular intervals, to see which conditions suit them best. I'm not convinced that any of them will actually develop, but if they do, I'll have to study that development very carefully."

"If they grow into trees," Mercy judged, "it'll take a very long time. It'll be frightfully boring."

"Perhaps it will," Tom conceded, "but that remains to be seen. They might well be animals rather than plants. In any case, some trees grow very rapidly—some species of bamboo, for instance, can grow three feet in a day, an inch in less than an hour. Until I cut one up, I can't be sure whether or not they're seeds. They could be pupae of some sort."

Mercy was inquisitive, and took an interest in natural history, partly because there was relatively little else of interest in the grounds of Andersley. She knew what a pupa was. "You mean they might split and butterflies might come out?" she said.

"It's unlikely," Tom said, "but not impossible."

"Or dragons?" Mercy suggested.

"Even less likely," Tom told her.

"But not impossible," she said, springing the trap that he'd carelessly set for himself. How could he rule anything impossible, in the circumstances?

"I really don't know," he said, "but I'm eager to find out—that's why I want to get up early. Go to sleep now, like a good girl."

Mercy apparently decided that she had tested her father's patience long enough. "Good night, Daddy," she said. Tom reflected that it was not a familiar term of address that he would ever have been allowed to employ in the Old Earl's day, especially not if he had been caught reading in bed when he had been told to go to sleep.

"Good night, Mercy," Tom said, dutifully. He turned her lamp right down, but did not extinguish it completely. So far as he knew, Mercy had never shown any sign of a fear of the dark, or having nightmares— for which he was profoundly glad—but she always slept with a night-light, just in case.

He was glad, as he closed her bedroom door quietly, that he had taken the trouble to look in on her. Today, of all days, talking to Mercy gave him a slight thrill of contentment, like a metaphorical night-light in a dark world . . . but he knew that it could not protect him from nightmares, and there was always an irrational fear lurking at the back of his mind that if he spent too long in her company he might somehow infect her with the sickness in his soul, that he might spoil her somehow, and not in the way that the word was usually used in regard to children.

I have to keep Oates away from her, he thought. *Mealtimes are safe enough, while etiquette provides a shield of sorts, but she mustn't get close to him. I don't want her playing games with him on the lawn. Helen will keep her away, though; she senses the danger too.*

Oddly enough, though, Tom slept quite peacefully, for once. In spite of having had such a remarkable day, surely containing more than enough imaginative fuel for a whole sequence of nightmares, his slumber was calm and untroubled, and he woke up feeling genuinely refreshed, for the first time in months . . . or years. His mood, as he went down to breakfast, was almost good.

V

HELEN was alone in the dining room.

"I've told Janet not to disturb your friend," she said, "and to let him wake up in his own time. I looked in on Mercy, but she was fast asleep too. Did I hear you talking to her last night?"

"Her light was on," Tom said, apologetically. "I just looked in on her to say goodnight. I only stayed for a minute."

"I'm not complaining," Helen assured him. "My light was on too, I believe, but you didn't look in on me."

Tom looked down at the two boiled eggs that had just been placed on his plate as Maggie rushed in after hearing the door open and close. Although doubt-less freshly-laid, they were hard-boiled, having been prepared earlier, and the toast in the rack was cold. It would never have been tolerated in the Old Earl's day, but the Old Earl was dead and buried, and had shown no sign as yet of haunting the manor in order to provide a spur to the renewal of standards.

"I assumed that you were reading," he said. "I didn't want to interrupt—and we'd already said goodnight."

"Considerate, as always," Helen commented, without making the sarcasm ostentatiously evident. "I assume that you'll be rushing off as soon as you've finished breakfast?"

Tom picked up the cup of coffee that had just been poured. That, at least, was still lukewarm, but it tasted suspiciously as if it had been thinned out with chicory. Again, that would have made the Old Earl—no stranger to Camp Coffee—apoplectic with indignation, if it had managed to get to the front of his queue of annoyances, which had usually been fairly long by eight a.m., even in the days of perfectly-timed eggs, accompanied by crisp bacon, warm toast with orange marmalade and the occasional Grimsby kipper.

"I want to get on with the dissection," Tom confirmed. "I'm curious to know what I might find inside the mysterious seed." He kept talking, fearing that if he stopped, he might invite more veiled sarcasm. "The external structure suggests that it might be just a bag of storage-protein, but I can't tell for sure until I cut it open to see, and even if it is, there will doubtless a minuscule embryo tucked inside, waiting to begin consuming the bulk. The appearances are ambiguous, though; it might well be more like a pupa than a bean—but appearances are often deceptive when dealing with something new, so it might be something else entirely. I can't even tell whether our ready-made categories of plant and animal are appropriate in this instance.

Helen seemed glad to find him in a relaxed and talkative mood for once. "Where on earth did Oates get them?" she demanded.

"I don't know," Tom replied, honestly enough, and not wanting to raise the question of whether Oates had got them on Earth at all.

"How did he get them here with his feet in that awful condition?"

"I don't know," Tom repeated, but added, lest the repetition become infuriating: "I did ask—but he couldn't tell me. All he could say was that, wherever he had been, it was dark. He seemed to be coming from the direction of the old coal-pits, and there was mention of a labyrinth. Beyond that, your guess is as good as mine—but I'd rather you didn't harass him with questions. Leave it to me, please . . . and try to ensure that Mercy doesn't pester him with questions either."

Helen looked at him long and hard, radiating dignified disapproval. After a long pause for thought, she said: "Will you be able to get them to grow, do you think?"

Tom didn't know that, either, but repetition was becoming tedious even for him. "I'll do my best," he assured her. "I'll do everything I can. I need to succeed, if it's humanly possible."

It seemed to be on the tip of Helen's tongue to ask why, but she didn't. Tom assumed that she thought she knew why. She knew that growing things had become the last redoubt of his sense of purpose, his *raison d'être*, his final defense against the pressure of expectation, the only activity in which he could absorb his attention in order to find a measure of peace and solace that inactivity and the mundane duties of administering the estate refused him. Presumably, he thought, she would have preferred it infinitely if the last redoubt of his self-possession had been estate management, or, more narrowly, the house—or, more narrowly than that, the house*hold*: the family—but she must know that he couldn't help it. She appeared to have begun to doubt that he loved her, even that he had ever loved her, but she had to know that he would not have retreated as far as he had from life if he had been able to help it. She had to know that deep down, he still loved her, and always had . . .

Or had she? Perhaps she simply could not muster that kind of conviction.

Tom did not doubt that his wife had forgiven him, thus far, for his derelictions—even Mercy had observed that—but would she . . . could she . . . continue to forgive him if things did not improve? That, he did doubt. From her viewpoint, Oates was doubtless a complication she could have done without, and perhaps one too many—but she must suspect, must she not, that from Tom's point of view, Oates was something of a godsend, and that even if he had been sent by the Devil instead, he had something to offer that Tom needed: seeds of hope.

According to Oates himself, they were bloodthirsty seeds from beyond the Mountains of Madness, but still, they offered scope for discovery, perhaps scope for wonder, perhaps even scope for revelation.

Madness really had become mountainous of late, Tom thought: dangerous and forbidding, but strangely magnificent and almost sublime, magnetic in spite of its murderousness, not drab and not leaden.

"The servants can cope with Captain Oates," Helen said, obviously more to reassure herself than Tom. "They coped with the sanitarium; this is just an extension of that. No matter how creepy they find him, they'll put a brave face on it. I'll see to that. They've done it before. They have it easy, now that there's only three of us to look after, after the hectic days before the War. One last traumatized cripple won't change that. We can all cope."

Before the War, Tom recalled, the house had had a domestic staff of seventeen, and the ground staff, including the stable-lads, had numbered nine. Now, the domestic staff was reduced to six and the ground staff to two—not counting Alice, Sally and Maureen— one section of the stables having been converted into garages and equipment-sheds. Everything was shrinking—the family most of all, now reduced from more than ten to three. Not all the missing were dead, of course; some had simply moved on, but the effect was much the same; it was all part of the catastrophe, all a cause for mourning. Relatively speaking, though, the present staff did have it very easy, by comparison with what the pre-war staff had had to cope with, in terms of the demands put on them by permanent residents and infrequent guests. Diminished or not, they could certainly cope

The family's wealth had diminished markedly too, although Tom still had enough to meet his own modest demands. The Old Earl had been fond of saying, repeatedly, that land was the only true wealth, but Tom knew now that he had been wrong; once upon a time, the statement had been accurate enough, but the only true wealth nowadays was money—which, in spite of the persistence of the gold standard, had become a mercurial phantom deprived of any real substance. The idea that land was anything any longer but a sticky, filthy matrix for trenches, for battles, for bloodshed . . .

Tom stopped that train of thought in its tracks.

"I'm going out to the greenhouse now," he told Helen, after a pause in order to finish his coffee. "I'll call in at the study to pick up the seeds."

"You ought to wait for Oates," she said. "He'll surely be down in a minute and he'll need a good breakfast, to help him get his strength back. He didn't eat much at dinner—probably too tired."

Oates came into the room at that moment, looking slightly uncomfortable in an old, ill-fitting hunting-jacket and baggy trousers that did not belong to the suit that Tom had offered him. Tom realized that they were some of Jack's old clothes, which Janet must have found for him, having judged that Jack and Oates were a similar height.

It doesn't matter, Tom thought. *There are overalls in the greenhouse, and lab coats. I'll soon have him looking the part.*

"Good morning, Lady Andersley," Oates said. "You're right, of course—I was very tired last night, but I'm refreshed now, having slept very well. I hope you don't mind, but I got up early and asked Janet to send up some bread and cheese to my room, with a pot of tea. I'm ready to make a start when you are, Linny."

"I don't mind in the least," Helen said. "You must treat the house as your own while you're with us. But you ought to have let Tom take a look at your leg and your feet before getting dressed."

"There's no need," Oates assured her. "I'm healing well now. Janet has found me a pair of good boots, which fit almost perfectly, but I'll be careful not to put too much stress on my feet."

Jack's boots, thought Tom. *But Jack wouldn't mind. As I remember it, he rather liked Titus.*

"Let's go, then," Tom said to his friend—but, stung by a sudden imp of whimsy, he couldn't resist the temptation to say to Helen: "We might be gone for some time." In order to make it sound more like an innocent remark than a macabre joke, he added: "But don't worry, we'll certainly be back for dinner."

He led the way, and ushered Oates into the tropical greenhouse, closing and bolting the door behind them.

"This is it," he said, with feigned modesty.

Oates looked around, and then walked around, studying the trees, most of which were young, although a few of them were mature, towering over him even though he was a tall man. The oldest would have reached the panes of the arched roof of the greenhouse by now had Tom not pruned them with the utmost care in order to restrain their vertical thrust

"Very impressive," Oates said. "I recognize the bananas and the pineapples, obviously, but I don't think I've run across the round yellow fruits before. Breadfruit?"

"That's right. *Artocarpus*—a staple food in the Pacific, spread throughout the islands by ambitious colonists in primitive canoes long before Westerners began their own colonial crusade. We work on a larger geographical scale, though; nowadays, there are plantations of breadfruit in Asia, Central America and Central Africa. The breadfruit tree is one of the great successes of *acclimation*, although not as conspicuous as banana trees. Those sustain entire so-called republics, but the fruit has been in very short supply in England recently. Joseph Banks once hoped that breadfruit would become the manna of the British Empire, but most of the Africans transplanted to the Americas by the slave trade refused to eat it, defeating the rational crusade with their stubborn prejudice. It can be eaten raw, but it's more usually baked or fried, and often ground into flour—hence its name."

"These were the plants that provoked the mutiny on the *Bounty*?" Oates queried, indicating the breadfruit trees.

"No," said Tom. "The mutiny was just a mutiny, organized by a petty aristocrat who felt slighted because he thought his naval rank unjustly low; the breadfruit was only an excuse. Bligh subsequently collected more trees in the *Providence*, and completed his mission, after successfully navigating the small boat in which his loyal officers were set adrift across the Pacific. He was a brilliant man, fully deserving of his Royal Society medal, but the vilest of the mutineers, desirous of avoiding hanging when he returned to England, wrote a fictitious, self-serving account of the voyage, which, unfortunately, sold well, was widely believed and blackened Bligh's name. Botanists have always attracted ridicule and hostility, in spite of the vast contribution they've made to human progress and civilization."

Oates laughed. "That's my old Linny," he said. "I've heard it all before, remember—you're preaching to the converted. But don't stint yourself . . . I'll be very glad to hear it all again; it'll make me feel at home, even more so than sleeping in the best guest bedroom again, and renewing my acquaintance with dear Janet. Your wife, by the way, is a marvel. Did you woo her with flowers and scientific lyricism?"

Tom controlled an impulse to scowl. "I didn't woo her at all," he said. "That wasn't the way things were done, under the Old Earl. He decided that it was time for me to marry, once I'd won my spurs in the dragoons and decided to resign my commission; he shopped around for an eligible girl and asked for her hand on my behalf. I was lucky to be introduced to her before the wedding—but she is, as you say, a marvel. I fell for her immediately. It's probably not the only reason I have to be grateful to the old monster, but it's the one that springs most readily to mind. I'm sure we'd be very happy if the bloody War hadn't got in the way."

Oates' marred face showed evident consternation. "Sorry, Linny," he said. "I assumed that you were . . . very happy, that is. Charming little girl, too—sure to be as lovely as her mother one day."

"Sure to be," Tom echoed, colorlessly.

Oates immediately changed the subject, aware of having accidentally touched a nerve. "You've got the seeds," he said. "Let's unwrap them, shall we, and get down to business. Did you order some blood to mix with the soil?"

"Yes," said Tom. "One of the groundsmen fetched it from the abattoir at first light—only one bucketful, but it should be more than enough to start us off. It's in the corner by the door."

Before mixing the ox-blood with the mulch, Tom sat down at the table where the microscope and the microtome had pride of place. He selected the smallest of the seven seeds, split it carefully in two with a razor, and then placed one half in the microtome in order to produce thin slices suitable for staining and microscopic examination. During the staining he carefully sectioned the other half of the seed and selected a dozen sections for placing in nutrient solutions in Petri dishes, in the hope that some might grow there vegetatively. He was careful to add a few drops of blood to six of the nutrient solutions.

"What's the verdict?" Oates asked, when Tom had put the first few stained slides under the microscope, one by one—by which time the sun had risen far enough into the sky for the mirror reflecting and concentrating its light to produce an image as perfect as the device was capable of providing.

"None, as yet," Tom told him, dully. "No visible membranes, let alone walls, and no recognizable protoplasmic microstructures. The tegument is uniform, the pulp only slightly differentiated—seemingly acellular . . . very peculiar."

"I'm not following you, Linny: too much jargon."

"It's really quite simple," Tom said. "Complex organisms, whether plants or animals, are constructed of cells; they begin life as a single cell, which divides over and over again, and some of the daughter cells then differentiate, becoming specialized and organized into functional tissues. Plant cells usually have walls, which define the structure of the whole organism, whereas animal cells usually have more flexible membranes. Within most cells there's a nucleus and various subsidiary structures, or regions, in which the metabolic activity of the cell is organized.

"I can't see any of those typical features in the flesh of the things you've brought me. All earthly life, so far as we know, is related, part of a single evolutionary sequence extending, as the saying has it, from monad to man, and that makes earthly life-forms recognizable, in their fine structure, with the aid of microscopes. There are all sorts of anomalies and peculiarities, but fundamentally, the same building-blocks are identifiable. Not here. I can't find differentiated cells; the basic organization appears to be filamental—stringy, if you prefer. Earthly life is replete with filaments, of course, including tiny ones that are essentially long, thin single cells, but these things seem to me to resemble exceedingly long balls of string, entwined in complicated ways. Its structures, insofar as they can be seen, don't seem to have been built by gluing calls together in complex patterns, but by weaving knots and tangles in an infinite thread."

While Tom spoke, he fed more slides to the microscope, one after another, but they only served to confirm his initial impression.

Oates was unimpressed. "So they're not really plant seeds?" he queried. "Does that mean they're like eggs?"

"No," Tom said. "Unless I'm drawing mistaken inferences from poorly-prepared or ruined slides, these things originate from an evolutionary sequence unlike the one that produced life as we know it. If a spider's web were alive, and initiated an evolutionary sequence, it would probably do so by dividing into more webs, initially conserving the same pattern but eventually beginning to differentiate, to produce variant patterns. It would have probably have kept expanding, become more labyrinthine, evolving, as it were, *topologically* rather than arithmetically or geometrically. It might eventually have produced separate webs, by detaching particular substructures, but they would follow a pattern of evolution quite different from the evolution with which we're familiar. Some similar process appears to have produced the organisms with which we're dealing."

"And you can tell that simply by slicing one of the damn things up and looking at it under a microscope?" Oates seemed skeptical. Tom could hardly blame him.

"I could be wrong," he said. "I'm drawing inferences from limited and puzzling data. The Old Earl would just have put his forefinger to his temple and said: "Doolally tap"—but he was a Victorian, who refused to believe in evolution and had been brought up to think that Thomas Huxley and Herbert Spencer were the Devil's minions. He thought that men—men like him, that is, because he was in two minds about women and blacks—had been created in God's image, and that if they really were made of cells, then it was because cells were part of that image . . . and hence that if these entities aren't made of cells, they're essentially ungodly, evil incarnate."

Tom stood up then, placed six pots on the table, one by one, and started gathering materials with which to fill them: matrices of various make-up and texture, laced with ox-blood at various dosages. While he worked, methodically and almost mechanically, Oates said: "You're telling me that these plants—let me call them plants for want of anything better—aren't from Earth? That they're from some other planet?"

Tom thought it interesting that his friend had jumped so readily to that conclusion, almost as if he already knew that to be the case.

"Not necessarily," he said. "All I'm saying is that, in my judgment, they might belong to an evolutionary sequence different from the one that produced all the organisms around us, which came from the sea to colonize all the land. Perhaps ours wasn't the only evolutionary sequence to begin in the depths of the sea, and this one only began to colonize the land at a much later phase of prehistory, unobtrusively. Perhaps it began somewhere else, under the surface of the Earth, not ultimately dependent on the energy of sunlight, like all the life we know, but drawing its elementary energy supply from the heat of the earth's core—and again, beginning its eventual colonization of the surface slyly and unobtrusively. That is, after all, how evolution proceeds: by complexification, differentiation, and colonization. That's its essence."

"It wasn't just the Old Earl who didn't like you saying things like that, was it?" Oates remembered. "It didn't go down too well at Eton, either. By the time you and I were there, the days when all the teachers had to be in Holy Orders were long gone, but the culture lingered. Evolution was on the curriculum, but the masters tied themselves in knots arguing that it didn't contradict the teachings of the Church of England. But you wouldn't stand for that, would you? You weren't content to be a wishy-washy agnostic; you were determined to be a vociferous dyed-in-the-wool Atheist. You learned to hold your tongue eventually, but I know what a strain that put on you. I sat beside you on the bench while you fulminated, and I was the audience for your secret sermons. God, I remember that as if it were yesterday, whereas the last . . . seven years, according to you . . . is mostly a blur."

"You were very tolerant," Tom said. "I don't think I'd have got through it if I hadn't had your steady support and generous ear . . . which I appreciated all the more because I knew that I never converted you, that you simply didn't care whether I was right or wrong, but only that I was your friend."

"It wasn't that I didn't care," Oates said. "Just that . . . . . . well, if you were wrong, I thought you were entitled to be wrong. I never believed in caning boys for the sin of heresy. I always thought that the Boers and the blacks were entitled to be wrong too, if they were wrong, and that even if Kitchener and his ilk were right—which I never really believed—it didn't entitle them to prove it with rifle bullets. I was sick of it. That's why I joined the Terra Nova expedition: no enemy except the ice, I thought, heroic endeavor without murder. But I reckoned without Scott: just another Kitchener in disguise .... he killed us all with his recklessness and lousy planning, while boasting all the time about what a hero he was and what good chaps we were for supporting him in his lunacy. I was so angry, at the end, when I stormed out of the tent; if there'd been anything to be gained by killing him instead of myself, I'd have done it—but my leg and my feet were so bad that I was effectively dead already . . . except that, somehow, I wasn't . . . and now my feet and my leg are healing, miraculously. I'd thank God if I were in any other company, but you wouldn't approve, would you, Linny?"

Tom laughed, briefly, still moving like an automaton as he plunged the six remaining "seeds," one by one, into the various bloody matrices. Ideally, he should have withheld the blood from one in order for it to serve as a control, but he had decided not to take the risk, and merely to vary the dosage of the blood in the hope of being able to calculate an optimum even with an inadequate sample.

"No, Titus," he said. "I wouldn't disapprove. The most valuable thing I learned at Eton was what you taught me: that the other boys, and the masters, and even Lord Kitchener and the Old Earl, if they were wrong, were entitled to be wrong, and that there was no point getting angry about it. You taught me to leave unrighteous wrath, the plaything of simple minds, to God and his minions. So no, Titus, I don't mind you thanking God at all, for what seems to you to be a miracle."

"It doesn't seem to you to be a miracle?" Oates queried, mildly. "I'm back from the dead, but it doesn't seem to you to be a miracle?"

"No," Tom said. "The word miracle is an empty concept. To say that something inexplicable is miraculous is a tautology. I'm content to think that your reappearance is inexplicable, and all the more interesting for that. Whoever is responsible, it wasn't God. God is another empty concept, which merely provides the illusion of an explanation—and, of course, a fake justification for the unrighteous wrath of simple minds, extending all the way from the Eton cane to the massacre on the Somme."

"That's the old Linny," Oates said. "It does me good to hear you. You're right, of course. In my case, it wasn't God, it was the barrel-boys . . . but I doubt that they're responsible for all the other miracles . . . and if you're right, I suppose they can't be henchmen of the Devil either . . . which is a relief. No possibility, then, of these things hatching out the beasts of *Revelation*?"

Having finished his experimental potting, Tom stood back to survey his handiwork and then glanced sideways in an attempt to ascertain that Oates' remark wasn't serious.

"No, Titus," he said. "No possibility at all."

"Good," said Oates. "Yesterday, though, you did mention the Last Trump and Judgment Day."

"Figuratively speaking," Tom emphasized. "Perhaps you have been resurrected, somehow, but not in response to any angelic clarion call."

"No," Oates agreed. "The barrel-boys have mouths of a sort, I think . . . but they don't play the trumpet, or the harp." The observation seemed to discomfit him slightly, and he changed the subject abruptly. "God isn't only employed as a justification for righteous wrath, Linny. The padre in the Inniskillings, if you remember, wasn't a tub-thumper. He was always telling us that God is love."

"Just an example of muddled thinking," Tom told him, sternly. "When men invented gods—and I do mean men, not humans—in order to fill an imagined void in their minds, which weren't sufficiently sophisticated to accommodate voids, they saw them first and foremost as punishers, always venting their wrath on poor hapless humans and in constant need of appeasement. They could only imagine chosen people as people who were occasionally let off punishment, people who did everything in their power to avoid attracting punishment—mostly sneaks and cads rather than the genuinely virtuous, who knew that the commandments were a sick joke intended to torment people. But as life gradually became easier, thanks to the sons of Cain, they learned the lesson of remorse and they invented a different god, quite unlike the father figure of the Old Testament, whose prophet preached kindness and forgiveness. It never caught on, of course, but it taught the great lesson of everlasting hypocrisy.

"Gods were, of course, the personification of human emotions, and the emotion of wrath was easily understood, easily felt and easily visible, exemplified in fatherhood. Love was the motherly counterpart, but elevating a mother to the status of a god was something that only a few relatively meek peoples could do, and they were mostly exterminated by their wrathful neighbors, so that was where Christians exercised the gift of hypocrisy to the full, allowing a mother to be the mother of a god, but only if she could be a virgin, unpolluted by the primal wrath of sexual violation. Male attitudes to women were confused before that, of course, but while wrath was the only God and masculinity was his prophet, women, as objects of primal wrath, were reduced to the status of property, like domestic animals. With the invention of a god of love—not a god of lust, like the old Aphrodite, but a god of kindness and forbearance—the situation became deeply confused and paradoxical. He became a victim of wrath, in order that people . . . I mean men . . . could feel remorse for having crucified him, and in order that the gift of hypocrisy could be extrapolated to its perverse maximum—but what can you expect from the sons of Abel?"

"You obviously haven't mellowed in middle age, Linny," Oates observed, "but I'm not sure that I ought to be glad to see that. Remind me of your version of the allegory of Cain and Abel, will you? It's become a little hazy, although I remember it earning you a caning once, and you saying afterwards—to me if not to the master—that in any sane fabulation it ought to have been called an abeling. I never quite got the joke, I'm afraid."

"It's simple," Tom said. "In the Bible story, Cain was an agriculturalist, a grower of crops—a botanist, in essence—whereas Abel was a herdsman, whose flocks produced meat. They both made sacrifices to God, but God, like the murderous carnivore he was . . . is . . . preferred Abel's sacrifice. Then Cain became indignantly wrathful and slew his brother—of which, for some reason, God didn't approve, even though wrath and slaughter were very much his things, and Cain was cursed. And the curse has continued through the ages, stigmatizing and belittling all growers of crops and botanical explorers, although their endeavors in turning meager wild plants into bountiful harvests by means of careful selection and patient nurture, have enabled the human race to enjoy all the wealth of nature, whereas nomadic herdsmen like Abel became violent plunderers and invaders, massacring their agrarian brothers. So, the sons of Abel are men like Genghis Khan, Tamerlane and Attila the Hun, whereas the sons of Cain are men like Joseph Banks, Charles Parmentier and William Bligh. Men, of course, being what they are, somehow make Cain an incarnation of evil and Abel a hapless victim—which only goes to prove the awful extent of human unreason."

"Yes," said Oates, "I remember now. You really did . . . do . . . have your own way of looking at things. What does Helen think of all that?"

That was an embarrassing question, which Tom hesitated to answer. Eventually, he said: "I haven't read that particular sermon to her. In fact, I've only recited it to a handful of people since leaving Eton, and not to anyone since coming home. It seemed . . . kinder. If that makes me a hypocrite, so be it."

Oates nodded. "And when are you going to recite it to Mercy, by way of education?" he enquired, with the ghost of a smile on his as-yet-unhealed lips.

"I don't know," Tom said. "When she's ready, I suppose."

Oates looked around, at the trees. "So you're a son of Cain," he said, "quietly growing bananas and breadfruit, having done your share of killing in the Inniskillings . . . but you didn't kill your brothers, did you? That's one thing you don't have to feel remorseful about."

"No," said Tom, "I didn't kill Jack and Hal . . . or father, or the Old Earl . . . but that doesn't mean that I can't feel a measure of remorse. I have the title, after all . . . I'm an earl, just like Kitchener. I can't evade my share of the responsibility . . . for Jack and Hal, the Boers and the blacks, and more Germans than I can imagine, let alone count. My personal contribution of lethal bullets was very meager, but I was an integral part of it. I still am."

"So growing bananas is a kind of penance?" Oates suggested. "Not that I have any right to criticize, given the absurd form that my penance took. At least yours is useful. Why bananas, though?"

"Why not?" Tom retorted, although he could have explained in far more detail, and would probably have enjoyed giving the explanation. Although Oates was not showing the slightest evidence of hostility, though, he felt as if he were under attack and he wanted to damp the discussion down. It was his own fault. Until Oates had asked him directly, he had never given any thought to the fact that he had never given Helen his Cain and

Abel lecture, and thus had never had to ask himself why he had not done it. It laid uncomfortably bare an element of his shame, his disapproval of himself, and his notion of the truth. But he didn't hold it against Titus, who was only doing what he had always done, back in the old days: keeping him balanced, keeping him calm. It was, on the whole, a good thing that he had come, a good thing that he was here, even if he had arrived by labyrinthine ways from some kind of underworld, bringing with him seeds, or spores, or pupae that might yet prove to be the Beasts of Revelation in embryo.

V

TOM and Oates soon settled into a routine, spending their days in the tropical greenhouse, ostensibly working, although, in truth, they were mostly simply waiting, there being nothing to do except leave the "seeds" to their own devices. Tom sometimes had to leave Oates to his own devices too, while he attended to various kinds of unavoidable estate business, but Oates didn't seem to mind, perfectly content to remain on watch in the greenhouse, tending to his charges with a quasi-maternal affection. He came to dinner every evening in the house, and engaged in polite conversation with Helen and Mercy, but he made no attempt to associate with Helen at other times, and he always evaded Mercy's occasional suggestions that he play with her on the lawn. Tom felt sorry for her, when he saw her pitching a baseball at a tree-trunk for want of a batter or a catcher, but he did not volunteer to fill the gap in her endeavor. He told himself that she wasn't ready for it yet, although he knew full well that he was lying: that he was the one who wasn't ready, and didn't even know why.

He tried hard, and succeeded after a fashion, in finding a way of thinking about the mysterious alien entities that seemed to make a kind of sense.

The pieces of "web" that he dissected from the sections of the sacrificed seed—the nature of which he dubbed a "Gordian knot" for the sake of convenience—didn't seem to be capable of "vegetative" reproduction, at least in the conditions that he provided, but they did seem to have some regenerative capacity, as long as they weren't cut up too small. The two seeds that he tried to grow in the hydroponic apparatus did nothing, even when bathed in blood and nutrients, and eventually, he transplanted them into pots, figuring that he needed to take every chance he could get under what seemed to be the better conditions.

Of the four planted in solid matrices from the start, only two made any progress at all in the first week—but two seemed better than none, and probably better than he had any right to expect, given the venturesome nature of his trials. But the two Gordian knots did grow, and grew as he might have expected, the threads making up their structure elongating, winding more intricately, and beginning to form strange loops that probably qualified as embryonic knots. He could not tell, by the end of that first week, what kinds of tissues the embryonic knots might eventually form, but he soon convinced himself that the form of the ensemble was not aiming to produce some kind of plant with roots, a stem and foliage, or some kind of vermicular animal. The best guess he could make was that the ensemble had a vague pentamerous symmetry, like a starfish or a sea-cucumber—echinoderms in general, in fact.

That first week was rather tense. No one else set foot in the greenhouse, although Mercy knocked on the door more than once asking to come in and see what was happening, and sulked when entry was refused. At midday, Maggie, the kitchen-maid, left a tray outside the door bearing a cursory snack, and Mercy tried to take advantage of its opening to obtain permission to enter, but Tom always sent her away. When the meal was over he put the tray back on the doorstep for Maggie to collect.

The tropical house was hot and damp, not exactly a healthy environment, but Oates didn't seem to have brought any infectious agents back from the dead, so Tom and he felt more comfortable there than they had in similar conditions in Africa while on route marches with the dragoons. Oates, in fact, seemed to be thriving in the conditions. The wound in his thigh had healed completely for a second time, according to his testimony, and his feet soon showed no sign of necrosis or blistering; none of his toes fell off, and he soon seemed to be walking normally, apart from the characteristic limp cased by the unequal length of his legs, which showed no sign of evening out. The most obvious change was, however, in his face. The damage had not been restricted to the dermal layers; the chill had also crept into the musculature. By the seventh day, however, the face had recovered its normal coloring and its muscles had recovered all their power of expression. Although he had not quite recovered his old handsome visage, Oates no longer seemed at all monstrous; he could have walked along the Headrow in Leeds without attracting any fearful or repulsed attention.

Tom felt that he was getting better in parallel. Talking about old times, as they routinely did, seemed to be helping both of them to adapt to their new selves—and while they were talking about old times, everything went smoothly. It had a frustrating dimension for Tom, though, because it certainly wasn't what he wanted to talk about *all* the time. As Oates recovered his old appearance, Tom got the impression that he was as eager to tell him about all the impossible things that had happened to him as he was to hear them, but something was inhibiting him, suppressing his memories, or at least the ability to bring them out into the open. Tom could understand that, after a fashion, because if and when the conversation shifted from Eton and Africa to the Ardennes or the Chemin des Dames, he found his own tongue freezing and his own mind shying away, especially from the catastrophe of the second Battle of the Aisne.

Tom made every effort to probe and prompt, as delicately and deftly as he could, and Oates made efforts too, but there really did seem to be things that he literally could not say, and not just for lack of an appropriate vocabulary. He was mentally alert, in full possession of his faculties, but it was as if he were under a spell of some kind. By the end of the first week, the two of them had made as little progress with Oates' story as they had with the task that the "barrel-boys" had apparently allotted to him as a condition of his return, but Tom had become more optimistic about the prospect of obtaining further clarification. Just as he had insisted on a degree of variation and gradation in the initial planting conditions of the seeds, he tried all kinds of maneuvers to figure out how to help his friend's memory grow and develop.

The whole point of a *jardin d'acclimation*, he told himself, was to test different environmental conditions, in search of the optimum, in advance of the dogged struggle to train subsequent generations of plants to adapt to different and varying conditions. With only seven specimens, one of them sacrificed to microscopic analysis, Tom had not been able to plan a proper multivariable grid, but he had at least made sure that all the eggs weren't in one circumstantial basket.

Having given him all the advice he had to give, Oates was content to yield to his expertise thereafter—that, after all, was why he was at Andersley. The cultivation of his own story was, in Tom's mind, an analogical process. He approached it from different directions, carefully and methodically, in the hope of finding the most suitable matrix. *The one thing a practical agriculturalist—a true son of Cain—needs more than anything else,* he often repeated to himself, *is patience. Fallow land doesn't become cornfields overnight, and colonies aren't built in a day. Success is a matter of generations, of lifetimes, of taking the long view . . . while hoping that catastrophe will stay away.*

"I hope you didn't tell the barrel-boys that I have some kind of magical ability," Tom said to Oates, one day when things seemed to be proceeding far too slowly and not very well, in terms of the growth of the Gordian knots. "I don't have what the old gardeners used to call green fingers . . . and yours have lost the hints of green that you had when you first appeared on the driveway."

It was a joke of sorts, but not a good one—in fact, it was in rather poor taste—but Oates took it in his lop-sided stride.

"You do have a gift, Linny," he assured Tom. "I always knew that, even at Eton. The others ragged you about it, but they knew that you had a real affinity with plants, and that your herbals weren't just a pointless hobby, like a stamp collection."

"Nothing like a visible gift to encourage bullying," Tom observed, drily, "except, of course, a limp or similar affliction. You were lucky you didn't catch that bullet until you were half a world away from the old *alma mater*."

"I was ill a lot," Oates reminded him. "I had to leave in the end. But the other boys didn't add unduly to the suffering, and they didn't give you a particularly hard time either. They mocked, but they mocked everyone and everything. It was just the way things worked. It wasn't that bad."

He was right, Tom thought; it hadn't been that bad, but Oates deserved much of the credit for that. Isolated, Tom knew that he would have been dead meat, figuratively speaking; without Oates to sustain him—not just at school, where everyone died a little, but in the dragoons—he really would have gone doolally tap. Tom sometimes thought that no junior lieutenant could ever have required a sympathetic captain as much as he had, although Oates would have dismissed the idea immediately had Tom mentioned it. Tom knew how much he owed to Oates, but Oates didn't seem to, or didn't want to admit it.

"So," Tom said, when he was finally satisfied that four of the seeds planted out in the pots were developing, albeit at different rates, and that the partial success of Oates' mission seemed assured, barring disasters, "we seem to have found a viable matrix—perhaps not the optimum, but good enough. The structure of the more mature individuals is becoming more evident."

"They're starfish," Oates judged. "But they didn't like water, did they? Terrestrial starfish."

"More like brittle-stars, actually," Tom judged, "But that's a silly name, because the species it's applied to are very flexible, not at all brittle, Ophiruoids is the technical terms, so your fellows—our fellows—would be better nicknamed pseudo-ophiuroids."

"Too much of a tongue-twister for me," Oates replied. "I'll stick to starfish, if you don't mind . . . vampire starfish. It has a nice ring to it, don't you think?"

Tom didn't, but he avoided an explicit contradiction. "Probably best not to use that term with regard to Helen and Janet," he said. "I'll stick to pseudo-ophiuroids in my reports to them. It'll seem like gobbledygook, but they're used to that from me. If they ask for an explanation, I'll give them a brief lecture on echinoderms and their evolution."

"You'll be lucky to get away with blinding them with Latin," Oates opined. "It certainly won't wash with Mercy. My advice is to stick to starfish—but drop the vampire; I'll keep that just between us."

"I'll take it under advisement—although I'm not sure it's advisable to take advice on jargon from the man who invented 'barrel-boys.'"

"Obviously," Oates admitted, "you would have devised a far richer vocabulary had they brought you back to life, but 'barrel-boys' and 'minotaurs'—not to mention 'seeds'—were the best I could do, however inapt they might be. Sorry."

"You have nothing for which to apologize, Titus," Tom assured him, automatically, but added, by way of tentative probing: "Can you tell whether the barrel-boys find our progress so far satisfactory. I'm assuming that they have some way of monitoring it, of keeping in touch with you. Is that right?"

"They know," he said, confidently. "As to whether they're satisfied or not . . . I can't tell."

"How do they know?" Tom asked. "So far as I know, you haven't been anywhere near the old coal-pits, if that's where they're lurking, or anywhere else that there might be an entrance to a subterranean labyrinth."

"They can read dreams," Oates said.

"They can read minds?" Tom echoed, trying to sound more incredulous than he was. "All the way from Antarctica?"

"They can read *dreams*," Oates repeated, insistently. "Not minds. They can't track our conscious thoughts, but the unconscious is a different matter. That has a collective aspect to it; it's mostly our own but not entirely. I doubt that they can understand much of what they read, but they can respond to it. They can put ideas in our heads, although it's not always easy to for us to bring them up from the internal labyrinth. The well is too deep and the bucket is leaky."

It was the longest speech that Oates had ever made about the individuals that had sent him back from beyond the Mountains of Madness, dead or alive. Tom was eager to follow it up while the window of opportunity seemed to be ajar.

"But you can do it?" he queried. "You can lower a figurative bucket into the well of the unconscious, and bring back . . . ideas."

"I'm beginning to," he said. "I couldn't, when I first arrived; I slept far too soundly, but things are beginning to come back, and I'm beginning to get the hang of the recovery. It isn't really a leaky bucket, of course—that's just a metaphor—but there really is a well of sorts, and a labyrinth. I fell into it, when I stormed out of Scott's hut.

"I thought you fell into a crevasse?"

"So did I," he said. "That was the intention. I probably did—but I didn't reach the bottom. Somehow, I sidestepped, into the labyrinth . . . the world-labyrinth, that is, not the labyrinth of the unconscious mind, although the two ideas are linked. I'm sorry that I'm not good at explanation, Linny, but I'm as confused as Helen or Janet would have been, or anyone but a scholar. Anyhow, I carried on falling, although the world-labyrinth isn't like a vertical shaft, and it has no bottom. It's twisted and tangled, but once you're in it, gravity doesn't seem to work any more. I couldn't see anything, at first, or hear anything, but I could feel presences. Over time, it seemed that I adapted; I still couldn't see or hear with my eyes and ears, but I was able to dream. Gradually I got better at it."

"But you weren't dead, at least," said Tom.

"That is not dead which can eternal lie," Oates said, in a strange voice, almost as if he were reciting semi-consciously, "and with strange eons . . . I don't know that I was alive, but I was dreaming. I could still feel. I could still feel the cold. I still can."

Tom had had occasion to touch Oates on numerous times—his hands, and especially his feet—and he had always observed that the captain's body temperature seemed to be lower than his own. He might have thought of him as "cold-blooded," had he not, as a biologist, been keenly aware of the inaptitude of the phrase in application to exothermic reptiles. He had grown used to the phenomenon, and had stopped thinking about it. Whatever other gift he might or might not have, he had certainly acquired the gift of not thinking about things that he found disturbing.

"What else could you feel?" he asked.

"All sorts of things," he said, "but they were fragmentary; it was impossible to make sense of them—at first, anyway. But as the dream-fragments accumulated, I began to find patterns. I began to connect up the imaginative images, gradually to form pictures. At first, it was very blurred, but gradually, shapes began to form in the pattern of ideas. Some were actual visual images, but it wasn't like seeing with my eyes, more like viewing directly with my brain, as you can in dreams while your eyes are shut.

"It was a slow process, I think, but I didn't have much awareness of the passage of time, because it wasn't measurable. Bit by bit, though, I began to piece together a *story* of sorts. I might have made some of it up, but only to make connections, to fill in gaps. Much of it . . . most of it . . . came from outside, from *them* . . . or from somebody or something that was very interested in them, something that was trying to study them, to understand them."

"*Them* being the barrel-boys?" Tom prompted.

"Yes, but not just the barrel-boys. There are other . . . entities in the labyrinth. Several kinds of . . . Antarcticans . . . and others . . . not only minotaurs but minotaur-makers . . . the Arcticans are there too, lurking and hiding . . . There's a war in progress, you see . . . a war that's been raging for . . . I don't know, millions of years, at least, perhaps thousands of millions . . . strange eons, if you like. Not just here or there but everywhere. There are peaceful interludes, I think, when everything calms down, and stops . . . but it always starts again, eventually, and it never *really* stops."

"It's the way of the world," Tom observed. "It's no different on the surface."

"So I gather," Oates replied, "although I know you don't like talking about your war, certainly not at the dinner table, where you and Helen put on such a practiced act of contented civilization, as if you were living in a microcosmic cocoon, albeit not a very comfortable one."

"We have to keep up appearances, for Mercy's sake," Tom objected.

"If you say so," Oates agreed, too polite to deny it forthrightly. "But whatever the reason, I do understand. Some things can be thought, but not said . . . and some things can't even be thought. Believe me, I know. Polite society requires self-censorship, in order to retain the varnish of civilization . . . but sometimes, the varnish cracks, and if it can't be repaired, the dam bursts, and violence ensues. All of that I understand, but that's by the by. I think, at last, that I've been able to string enough fragments of my nightmares together to shape a story. I think I can make a start on straightening out its labyrinthine twists—probably a much more necessary process than simply cutting it short, but I'll summarize as best I can, and try to put things in some sort of order. What will seem to you to be vague remains vague because it *was* vague, because I'm still vague myself, even though my face looks much clearer now than it did when I first looked into the mirror in the guest-room.

"So, to recap, I *did* fall into a crevasse—a seemingly bottomless crevasse. It should, in terms of mere earthly topography, have taken me down to a niche in the ice or rock, or into the sea, but it didn't. It took me to . . . how can I put it? . . . the Other Antarctica. I don't mean that in the trivial sense that there's an island, or an entire continent, buried under an expanse of ice, although that isn't irrelevant to the story. Once upon a time, you see, that submerged continent was warm—really warm, not merely less cold. It was a vast land with rivers, and forests, and fields, and cities . . . and mountains . . . but the ice has crushed all that. It has crushed everything . . . but it happened slowly, and the Antarcticans had time to react. They could have gone elsewhere, I suppose, heading for what are now the tropics, but they didn't. They reacted in their own way. They built the labyrinth.

The icescape looks so still now, so nearly eternal, but it's not still, let alone eternal, on the scale of barrel-boy experience and barrel-boy lifespans. Even now, the ice moves, still grinding and crushing, still twisting the labyrinth.

"There are still rivers and lakes underneath the ice in places . . . even life, apparently. If the ice were to disappear, as the ice that once covered Yorkshire disappeared, tens of thousands of years ago, the land would regenerate, just as Yorkshire has. Well, not *just* as Yorkshire has, because Yorkshire was only covered for a few tens or hundreds of thousands of years: a mere eye-blink of geological time, let alone cosmic time. Antarctica . . . well, life would come back gradually there too, even to the crushed and scoured rock, but it would come back very differently, bearing very little resemblance to the Yorkshire of dales and wolds . . . and as well as the trivial Other Antarctica, there's a quite different and much stranger Other Antarctica, which also needs to regenerate, even though it's still there, slow but alive, and it's inhabitants are still dreaming. That regeneration will be a whole other story, with Mountains of Madness instead of wolds. The ancient mountains have been ground down to dust and flattened, but they still exist, in spirit."

"Like the Old Earl in Andersley," Tom joked—but Oates didn't laugh, and didn't show any evident sign of having heard what Tom had said. While he was trying to piece his story together, the far traveler had settled into a peculiar kind of reverie, as if he were letting his intelligence idle while his mouth ran on of its own accord. Tom suspected that that was the only way that Oates could talk about his experience, because doing so with his consciousness focused and concentrated would have activated the spell of sorts that was inhibiting his revelations. He was in a kind of dream-state, even though he was awake.

Tom didn't want to interrupt Oates again in case he broke up the flow, but he was a little worried, too, about letting the flow continue, because he was afraid that if it became too insistent, it might confront Oates' imagination with something indescribable, something unnamable and perhaps unthinkable, and confuse him utterly. Tom formed the conscious thought that he understood that, and could sympathize, but he knew that he was fooling himself. On the other hand, he thought, going with the flow while avoiding the worst potential obstacles seemed to be allowing Oates, at least for the time being, to skirt the truth, and thus to convey some expression of it without going into too much dangerous detail. Again, Tom told himself that he understood that, and sympathized, but he continued to doubt his own confidence.

All in all, though, it seemed to Tom that Oates *wanted* to explain. The captain was an Eton-educated officer, an intelligent man even if he hadn't been an academic star, and he needed to understand what had happened to him—and he wanted Tom to understand too, not just because Tom was his friend, and he needed him, but because he needed a sympathetic listener in order to help him get the story straight . . . and in order to extrapolate it beyond his memories, to try to figure out why he was at Andersley, and why he was growing weird alien organisms in the greenhouse.

The reverie resumed. "Imagine what a pickle we'd be in, Tom, here in north Yorkshire, if the ice were to come back," Oates mused, perhaps losing the thread of his previous argument but perhaps only following it through a kink in his mental labyrinth. "If there were people here before the last Ice Age, of course—Neanderthalers, I suppose—they would simply have retreated ahead of the ice, but they could do that easily enough because they were nomads, hunter-gatherers—Sons of Abel, in your allegory. They didn't have any elaborate agriculture, any cities or any concept of the ownership of land. The notion of opposing the ice, trying to fight it, would never have occurred to them. To you, though, a lord of the manor whose family has owned and farmed the land for centuries, the idea of retreat would be a very different matter, wouldn't it? You might be an exception personally, but think about the attitude that your grandfather would have struck. His immediate and stubborn impulse would have been to stand fast—to find a way of holding back the ice if he could, and if he couldn't, to find some way of living underneath it. Yorkshire folk are legendary for their stubbornness—even you share that trait, Tom—and it wouldn't just be the lords of the manor who thought that way. It would be everyone. You'd tunnel. You'd find a way, if there was any way to be found. You'd dig in."

No, Tom thought, *I wouldn't have. I'd have retreated, having learned my lesson at Mons and having had it hammered home on the Chemin des Dames. But that's not the point that Oates is trying to make. He's really talking about the Antarcticans, and why there's still an Other Antarctica, into which a hero like him could fall after storming out of Scott's tent, intent on keeping going, dead or alive.*

Oates confirmed that thought, without having read Tom's mind. "The things that once lived in Antarctica, a *very* long time ago," he said, "in one of the periods when it was warm, had the same kind of stubbornness as Yorkshire folk, and technological resources of which dalesmen and woldsmen can only dream. I don't know why they couldn't stop the ice—it's possible that the continental crust itself drifted over the Earths mantle, that it came to rest on the Earth's axis, having previously been located in kinder latitudes. Certainly, the Earth itself cooled, after a hot phase. Once, in a past remoter still, it had been completely covered in ice, and in one not quite so remote it had been entirely ice-free, but in the era I'm talking about—millions of millions of years ago, long before the life we know had even emerged from the sea to cover the land left vacant by yet another catastrophe—the ice was on the attack. Not just the ice, either; the Earth was a busy place in those days, with more than one kind of life—more than one kind of being, that is—fighting for its possession. Things seem quiet now, but we've only been here for an eye-blink of geological time, so we can't really tell, and if we could . . .

"Anyhow, the Antarcticans dug in. They retreated into the labyrinth. When they couldn't stop the ice, or decided not to stop it—because they might have decided not to, figuring that the ice might make a useful defensive wall against some other enemy—they tried at first to live underneath it, in lacunae and under the ground. Humans couldn't do that, obviously, because life of our kind is parasitic on sunlight: no light, no plants, and hence no food. The Antarcticans were different. They had other needs, other ways; they were no longer parasitic on sunlight . . . not, at any rate, to the same extent as us. They were highly intelligent, and I doubt that they ever imagined that they could establish any kind of stable situation that might endure for millions of years; they knew they'd have to keep on adapting, keep on changing . . . but that was their thing anyway. They were much more long-lived than we are, and they didn't think so highly of stability.

"We're mayflies," Oates added, drowsily, "and we dream of prolongation, of settlement, of consistency. They didn't see survival in those terms; they weren't utopians. They had strange and various resources, and they had strange and various methods too. They couldn't keep things going forever, maybe because of their other enemies, but when they settled for dormancy—not death but dormancy—in order to wait for more favorable circumstances to come around again, they left a great deal behind. The ice crushed a lot of it, over the course of hundreds of millions of years, but the residue had been designed to withstand that. Their enemies might have destroyed even more, or else the ones who were dug in and dormant might have suffered from some dire catastrophe of another sort—but still, the residue remained . . . and it still remains, much diminished, but still able, after a strange and distant fashion, to *survive*.

"The ice melted again—more than once, I think—but if that was what the sleepers were waiting for, it didn't trigger any mass awakening. I don't really have any idea what would . . . but there are some things I do know, or can imagine. The Earth isn't the only inhabited planet in the universe, by any means—there are millions, perhaps thousands of millions in the Milky Way . . . and some of them have evolved life-forms capable of traveling through space, and perhaps even through time. At any rate, our planet has been invaded more than once, by various species of star-spawn. Some of them are still here, but mostly dormant, like the Antarcticans . . . dormant and dreaming, mind, and still fighting wars in their dreams . . . petty wars that eventually get absorbed into *the* war, the World War. For that reason, and perhaps others, among the things the Antarcticans left behind were—and are—*traps*. Perhaps the traps had actually been disguised as crevasses, way back when, but that's definitely the way that some of them appear now. I fell into one. It was bottomless. I didn't smash my head on ice or rock, like poor Edgar Evans, and I didn't fall into the sea to be eaten by a leopard-seal. I just *fell*.

"Maybe I died and maybe I didn't die, but either way, I've come out of it again. *They* brought me out. *They* looked after me, as best they could, in ways that we probably can't understand. *They* communicated with me. Eventually, it appears, they sent me back. They let me go . . . at a price . . . and here I am."

VI

THAT evening, after dinner, Tom invited Helen to
go into the study with him, so that he could tell
her what he'd learned so far. Mercy wanted to come too,
and when her request was refused she asked Oates if he
would play ball with her on the lawn. Oates refused
too, politely, on the grounds that it was already getting
dark—because the nights were drawing in spite of the
effects of daylight saving time—and that he wanted to
read in his room, because he'd missed out on a lot of
books while he was away, and was still trying to catch
up. Mercy had to accept those excuses, but she flounced
out of the dining room in search of one of the servants
who was at a loose end, proclaiming that she wasn't
afraid of the dark, and had gone out after dark lots of
times before the armistice. The servants had orders to
humor her, but they didn't resent it; the younger wom-
en, in particular, were very fond of her.

"Oates' feet are completely healed now," Tom said,
when he and Helen were both comfortably seated.
"He's his old self again."

"I'll take your word for it," Helen said. She seemed slightly on edge, uncertain as to how she ought to take advantage of the rare opportunity to talk to her husband in private, but all she said in the end was: "How are the seeds coming along?"

"Two of the survivors are way ahead of the other two," Tom told her. "I've transplanted them all into the most hospitable matrix, but two haven't responded at all and two will take a while to catch up with the most advanced, if they ever do. The two that haven't responded will probably have to be written off, but Oates says that I shouldn't dwell on the failures, and concentrate on the successes."

"And do you have any idea yet what they are?"

"Nothing familiar. They now seem to me to be more like animals than plants, even though they show no sign of motility as yet. Their pentamerous symmetry is suggestive of echinoderms, and the way they're developing is reminiscent of ophiuroids, but that's just an analogy, a matter of convergent evolution."

"Long-legged starfish, you mean?" Helen was by no means scientifically illiterate.

"If you like," Tom conceded, grudgingly.

Her face did not give the impression that she liked it at all, but she passed on. "But they don't seem to be dangerous? No teeth, claws or stings?"

"Nothing detectable, thus far. But we have no idea how big they'll grow, or what sort of metamorphosis they might yet have to undergo. Their microstructure is labyrinthine, extremely convoluted, which presumably reflects their evolutionary sequence . . . ontology recapitulating phylogeny, in an approximate fashion quite different from the life-forms with which we're familiar. But that isn't what I wanted to tell you. Oates is loosening up, beginning to recover his memories and put them in some sort of order. He's given me the beginning of an explanation of what happened to him when he fell into the crevasse."

"And?" she prompted.

"He was collected by organisms of some kind, presumably a more mature branch of the evolutionary tree that produced the pseudo-ophiuroids for which he asked me to discover conditions of viability. They're extremely ancient, I think, perhaps derivative of an origin of life preceding the origin of our kind of life by thousands of millions of years, or perhaps derivative of a kind of life that was deliberately designed and engineered by highly sophisticated individuals of some sort. It seems that life might have evolved on Earth several times, as well as being supplemented by life that arrived here from elsewhere—star-spawn, as Oates puts it."

"All right," said Helen. "Whether we think that they're invaders from another star or not, it doesn't affect the fundamental problem. What do his so-called barrel-boys actually *want*? Of him, and of us?"

"They want us to develop the so-called seeds for them—which, for some reason, they can't do themselves, possibly because it's simply too cold where they are, but perhaps because they want it done clandestinely. They have enemies, apparently. All is not harmony in the dreamland labyrinth."

"Indeed not," said Helen. "Not if your night terrors are anything to go by. I can hear them, you know, even though you keep your door locked. Oates must be able to hear you too, when they're at their worst—and Mercy."

"I'm sorry," Tom said, defensively. "I thought they'd go away—at least, I hoped they would. For a while they were getting better, but lately . . . it *will* get better, I'm certain. But they have nothing to do with the pseudo-ophiuroids."

Helen left any doubts she might have about that unexpressed, for the moment. "But they managed to bring Oates here somehow," she observed, instead, in a scrupulously level voice, mimicking Tom's appearance of scholarly detachment. "Presumably, they could have transported him to a warmer climate, if they'd wanted to. Winter won't be long in arriving here, now that autumn is progressing."

"Just because they managed to bring him here, it doesn't mean that they could have taken him anywhere," Tom argued. "There's a physical labyrinth of some kind inside the Earth, apparently, but it's probably just a set of tunnels like those dug by moles, and its connections to the surface might be few and far between. The one he used might have led to a climate that's far from ideal . . . but they know about the greenhouse, and me."

"Good for you. Do they also know about me—and Mercy?"

"I don't think so. They know about me because Oates knew about me, and they eavesdropped on his dreams. Oates left for the Antarctic before I married you, and long before Mercy was born . . . and there's no reason to think that your existence and hers could be of any relevance to the entities that held him in suspended animation for so long, whether they're terrestrial or extra-terrestrial."

"There doesn't seem to be any reason any longer to think that we're relevant to you, either," Helen stated, flatly.

Tom winced, and remembered what Oates had said about the varnish of polite civilization so necessary to the maintenance of social cocoons occasionally cracking. "That's not the case," he objected, equally flatly. "You and Mercy are the most important things in the world to me."

"It doesn't show," Helen retorted. "But let's not argue about that. The matter in hand is the seeds . . . and Oates. Are the mysterious barrel-boys still eavesdropping on his dreams?"

Tom hesitated, but finally said: "I think so."

"So they could be aware of me, and of Mercy?"

"Only if Oates dreams about you," Tom replied, fully aware of the weakness of the reply.

"Is that why he avoids us?"

"No," said Tom, with a slight edge in his voice. "He keeps his distance from you out of politeness, because he knows that you're intimidated by his uncanny presence, and that you don't want him to have anything to do with Mercy."

"You mean that if it weren't for the prohibition that he thinks I've put in place, he'd be only too glad to let Mercy throw her precious baseball at him?"

That unexpected question left Tom at something of a loss. "I don't know," he said, "but I can't believe that it's a relevant issue. Perhaps he does dream about you, and about Mercy, now that he's apparently begun to dream again, after an interval, but I can't see how it can possibly be of any relevance to the entities that sent him here."

"You're probably right," she conceded, in a casual manner that was evidently feigned. "How about you? Would it be of any relevance to you if Captain Oates dreamed about me?"

Tom remember that Oates had gone on to say, mixing his metaphors, that once the varnish was cracked, the dam sometimes burst.

"He's a handsome man, after all," Helen went on, "now that he's recovered his looks. He's only a few months older than you, a certified hero, and single. And I've been . . . somewhat neglected of late."

Tom felt the blood draining from his face. He opened his mouth to say something, but no sound came out.

"You're both Old Etonians, of course," she added. "Officers and gentlemen. But tell me, how much do you think the code of gentlemanly behavior is really worth, in the face of temptation? As for the Old Earl, who negotiated our marriage so efficiently, what advice do you think he'd give me, in the present circumstances? Perhaps I can make a better estimate of that than you can. 'Your job is to produce a potential heir to the title, my girl,' he'd say—I know, because he said exactly that to me before the wedding, when Lilian was already dead and Josephine was showing signs of having flattered only to deceive. And he'd probably add: 'One way or another.' The one way doesn't seem to be working, does it?"

"Helen!" said Tom, finding his voice at last.

"My God," she said, "you really are shocked, aren't you? I can't blame you, I suppose. I really was celibate for all those years that you were away at the war, you know, waiting meekly for you to return home, like the perfect heroic wife I wanted to be. Opportunities weren't exactly prolific, of course, in a godforsaken hole like this, from which all the young men had been kidnapped by the army, but they weren't non-existent. But no; for four years I told myself: 'He loves me. Even though that old sod of a grandfather plucked me out of the hat for him, he loves me, far more than either of his brothers loved their luckless brides. When he comes home, everything will be all right. When he comes home, we'll take up where we left off. But everything wasn't all right, was it? And we didn't take up where we left off, did we? I was understanding, of course; I'd seen enough when I opened the house to the walking wounded, the permanently maimed and the hopelessly crippled, to know that the worst wounds from which the poor fellows were suffering weren't just in their flesh. But understanding can't last forever, Tom, and I very much fear that I'm beginning not to understand any longer. What should I do about that, Tom? I wish you'd tell me, because I really don't know."

After a long pause, Tom said: "I do try."

"I know you do, Tom," she said, in a voice hardly above a whisper. "That's the worst of it, in a way. If you had simply stopped caring, if you had simply begun to detest me, perhaps I could simply shrug my shoulders, pack my bags and take Mercy away figuratively if not literally . . . but to know that you do try, but that you're impotent to do anything, in more ways than one . . . that's hard. Because I loved you, in spite of the fact that you were forced upon me, and I wouldn't want to stop loving you, unless it's absolutely necessary. But I'm beginning to fear that it might be.

"We have to think about Mercy too—but have you noticed that her face doesn't light up any more, the way it used to, when you come into a room? She's a stubborn little girl; she won't stop coming to knock on the greenhouse door occasionally, even though you never open it, and she won't stop coming into your study when she knows that you're alone there, even though she knows that you'll only send her away. But how much longer do you think she can keep it up, Tom? How much longer do you think she can maintain her optimism, with no return?"

"I often go into her room to say good night," Tom said, defensively. "I think she sometimes stays awake and leaves her light on deliberately, no matter how late it is. She knows that I love her . . . and she understands that I'm busy during the day."

"No, Tom, she doesn't know, and she doesn't understand. She doesn't have the slightest idea what you do, or why you think it's so bloody important that you can never spare a moment for her . . . and quite frankly, nor do I. I sometimes leave my light on too, but you don't come in . . . because you can't face me when I'm in my nightgown. There will come a time, soon enough, when both of us will stop making the gesture and let the lights go out permanently."

Tom wanted to say "Please don't," but the words wouldn't come out. What right had he, after all, to make that request of her? What right had he, in the circumstances, to ask anything of her? He refused to ask himself what the Old Earl would have done, in the unlikely event of him ever being in a similar situation, or Jack, or Hal, because he had a good idea what the answer would be, and for himself, it would be no answer at all.

Eventually, he managed to say: "I'm sorry. You're right, it's been far too long. I should have pulled myself together months ago. I'll try . . . I really will."

"I know," she said. "I'm sorry, too, for trying to pressure you, but it really is becoming urgent."

"I do love you," Tom said. "I never stopped. I loved you at first sight, and I loved you all the more as we got to know one another. The War got it the way, but I never stopped, even for a moment, especially . . . in the trenches. I haven't stopped. I don't think I could, or ever shall."

"That's reassuring to hear," Helen told him. "I'd like to believe it. I'll try, but you might need to give me a little help. I'm sorry for putting you through that but . . . I couldn't hold it in any longer. I'll go to bed now—and don't worry, I won't leave my light on. Tomorrow, we

132

might both feel better. Good night, Tom.

She left without kissing him, and closed the study door behind her quietly. Tom would rather she had slammed it; the soft click made by the latch sounded strangely sinister.

But I can't help having nightmares, he thought. He wondered whether that was really true, and thought that perhaps he simply hadn't mastered the trick of it. *I survived Mons in '14, and I survived the Somme in '16. How many men were in both battles? Precious few, I'll wager. Why, then, should it have been the Chemin des Dames that did for me? It wasn't even a real battle—those new tanks simply rolled right over us like juggernauts; we were helpless, utterly impotent, too sick and dispirited even to put up a fight; it was a farce. Perhaps it was the ignominy of it. We had to retreat at Mons, but we regrouped. We stood our ground on the Somme, and my lads held our position, as we did in the first battle of the Aisne . . . but in the second, we folded like a house of cards. If the tank commander, unable to believe his luck, hadn't waited two days for further orders instead of pressing on to Paris immediately, so that when he eventually did move on he ran straight into those American farm-boys that Woodrow Wilson had sent over lickety-split, well-fed, well-armed and raring for a fight, it would have been a total disaster. It's no credit to me that it wasn't. But even so . . . why should that last straw have broken me, after I'd carried so many heavy bales so far? I couldn't have got through Eton, let alone the Transvaal, without Oates, but even so, I'm not a weakling. I have the medals to prove it . . . but they're just scrap metal. What I need is to be the husband that Helen needs, and the father that Mercy needs. Oates is doing his best to sustain me again, and has come back from the dead to do it, but it isn't working . . . yet.*

Pinning his hopes on that *yet*, Tom eventually went to bed himself, after telling Janet that he didn't need anything and that she could go to bed too, although it was still relatively early, in spite of the cloudy night being pitch black, with more than a hint of winter chill.

VII

THE next morning, Tom found frost-patterns on the window of his bedroom, but there were none on the panes of the greenhouse, the heat pumped out by the boilers maintaining the temperature inside at high level: heat that gradually seeped through the glass and kept the outer surface clean and bright.

Oates was already inside, and hadn't bolted the door, but Tom didn't scold him for that.

"Bad night, Linny?" Oates said, as Tom went to inspect the pots.

"Nothing serious," Tom assured him. "Just dreams."

That answer did not seem to reassure Oates in the least. "What kind of dreams?" he asked.

"Nothing serious," Tom repeated. "Nothing to do with these"—he indicated the alien flesh protruding from the bloody soil with a casual gesture—"and no sign of anything I'd be tempted to nickname a barrel-boy, an ophiuroid or a minotaur. Strictly personal."

"But you told Helen the story that I pieced together for you yesterday," Oates said. "I hope it didn't give her bad dreams."

135

"It didn't," Tom retorted, bluntly. "She has other things to think about too, you know. Vague ramblings about what might have happened in Antarctica millions of millions of years ago don't disturb her."

Oates didn't bother to point out that what had happened to him, seven years ago, enabling him to return from the dead, might be a different matter. Instead, he said: "I'm sorry that you and she are having . . . problems."

Tom stared at him. "What's that supposed to mean?" he said, sharply, although he knew perfectly well.

"Nothing," Oates lied. "I'm sorry I spoke. Not my place."

"No, Titus—I'm sorry I snapped. Please don't worry about Helen and me. We'll work out any difficulties. We have to, for Mercy's sake as well as our own. We know that—and so does Mercy, even though she's only seven. She's doing her best to help, even by being deliberately disobedient sometimes. We'll all pull together; we can't fail . . . unlike our precious pseudo-ophiuroids, two of which have already failed and two more seem to be struggling. Even there, though, two seem to be thriving. The barrel-boys *should* be pleased."

"They are," Oates told him. "If they're anxious, it's no reflection on you."

"Are they anxious?" Tom asked.

"I think so. They're nervous about the time factor. They know we can't go any faster, but they're worried that it might not be fast enough . . . that the starfish might not be mature in time."

"In time for what?" Tom asked.

"I don't know. Perhaps I should, but I don't."

Unable to make any further progress with that enigma, for the time being, Tom returned to his scrupulous observations of the alien creatures, made a few notes, and then started on his routine rounds of the fruit trees, examining and measuring the progress of the various fruits.

He soon lost track of time, which was partly the object of the exercise. He thought, wryly, that he had been trying to lose track of time for some while, before Oates had arrived at Andersley, without quite being aware of it—or perhaps just trying to give the time that was tracking him the slip. The tropical house had become a refuge, a redoubt where he had dug in, only coming out for dinner, to maintain an illusion of contact with Mercy, Helen and the world . . . and it had, he admitted reluctantly, been an illusion. He had talked to them, of course, and the servants too, especially Janet and Linda, but there was a sense in which, even when he had left the tropical house behind, he had still been dug in, peeping out through loopholes but not seeing very much. Now, thanks to the seeds from beyond the Mountains of Madness, he was dug in even further in his own home than he had been in the old chalk-pits under the Chemin des Dames . . . but he shied away from that comparison. He knew that he had to stop digging before he could make his way up to the surface again—and he had to do that soon, given Helen's ultimatum.

Unfortunately, he had no idea how much growing the pseudo-ophiuroids, and the story that surrounded them, still had to do before they reached the maturity that the barrel-boys seemed to be anticipating with anxiety, and what shape they might assume before he began—only *began*—to make a vestige of sense, not only of the pseudo-ophiuroids, but of everything.

It wasn't easy. Oates' benign presence in the greenhouse ought to have been helping, but the captain seemed to have lost something of his old charisma, even though he was his true self again. He had his once-familiar face again, handsome and debonair, but somehow, it was still slightly unhuman.

It's an illusion, Tom thought. *It's just because I know that he's been through something out of this world. The lack of humanity is entirely in the eye of the beholder.* Sometimes, however, he thought that because he was keeping such close company with Oates, he was becoming unhuman himself, and that wasn't a pleasant sensation.

Nevertheless, he kept reminding himself incessantly that the task he had been set was achievable. It wasn't quite understandable, as yet, but it was achievable, and he simply had to tell himself, if push came to shove, that he didn't have to understand it, he just had to do it, even if that made him reminiscent of an enlisted man and constituted thinking unbecoming of an officer.

*I'm just a donkey, he thought, or a camel, like Haig and all the rest. But I have no lions to lead any longer, if I ever did. There were certainly none left on the Chemin . . . but again he cut himself off. The point is, he re-*sumed, *that we did it. We all did it. And we all did our bit, just as everybody has to, in extreme circumstances. Paradox or not, it's only the unreal horrors that continue* *to horrify us. The real ones soon go beyond mere horror, and become life. They remain traumatic, still capable of turning the human unhuman, of contriving fates worse than death, but they cease to horrify us consciously . . . eventually.*

He was lying to himself.

He got the impression, sometimes, that Oates might be lying to himself too, that the story he was trying to let out was not merely something that was continually inhibited—presumably when he made contact with a truth that he wasn't supposed to reveal—but something that he could not face, and felt obliged to paper over, in order to deflect his consciousness. Sometimes, Oates would pause, temporarily unable to continue, as if his tongue had swollen in his mouth and stuck to his palate.

Sometimes, while he was listening, Tom felt strange frissons crawling through his flesh. Invariably, his clothing was damp with sweat, because it was so hot and humid in the greenhouse; the green leaves around him were dripping so profusely that it almost seemed to be raining indoors, but the fruit-trees didn't mind; they could bear it, and they relished it.

Oates, by contrast, didn't sweat. In spite of everything, he still felt cold to the touch. He did not complain of feeling cold himself—in fact, he seemed to relish the warmth and humidity of the greenhouse as much as the banana trees—but his body temperature was unnaturally low. The homoeostatic mechanism of his metabolism seemed to be keeping that temperature several degrees below the 98.4 Fahrenheit that was supposedly optimum for human flesh. Why?

When Oates confessed to any physical discomfort—which wasn't often, although his injured leg still caused him twinges, in spite of the thigh-wound having healed for a second time—Tom gave him a cordial to drink, in order to replenish his energy supplies as well as his liquid balance; it was something Helen and he had cooked up together. It seemed to help Oates feel better, but it didn't raise his body temperature.

Although his anxiety was manifestly increasing, Oates was able to continue his fragmentary account of the beings he called the barrel-boys. The fact that he had made contact with the billion-year-old Antarcticans, and had evidently made some kind of pact with them, seemed to Tom to imply that they were no longer dormant, but that wasn't the way that Oates represented it. The way he put it was that they *were* still dormant, or perhaps even dead—but that they were *very* good at dreaming. Humans were not, it seemed to them. Humans were mere infants by comparison, mere finger-painters, dream-wise. *They* could dream robustly even while dormant, perhaps even while dead . . . and their dreams were not confined to their physical bodies, having access, albeit in a limited fashion, not merely to the collective unconscious of their own species, but to those of certain other species, including humankind.

Tom attempted to prompt Oates repeatedly on the subject of the physical structure of the Antarcticans who had extracted him from their trap; the other was vague, but his descriptions gradually accumulated more detail.

"I began to think of them as barrel-boys," he explained, "although, like Eton nicknames, that was

deliberately chosen in a spirit of mockery and diminution—because their general shape reminded me somewhat of beer-barrels, with more complex organs at the
top and the bottom. They have five . . . well, let's call
them tentacles for want of a better term . . . at one end.
I don't know what to call the things at the other end,
and it would be taking Etonism too far to call them
'the scrapers at the bottom of the barrel,' although, the
phrase did occur to me. I'm reasonably sure that they
include sense-organs of a sort, and maybe a mouth at
the beginning of a gut . . . or maybe not. They're certainly not mere animals, although I couldn't think of them
as people, let alone rulers of an Antarctican realm, but
. . . well, let's just say that they're "dreamers" and leave
it at that.

"There are many other beings in the Other
Antarctica, obviously, including servants of the barrel-boys: slaves, or maybe domestic animals . . . some are
big, horrid things, swarming with tentacles and capable
of shapeshifting, like amoebae. I wasn't exactly told,
but I got the impression from dreams that might have
been intended to be informative that the domesticated
species had got out of hand at one point in the past—
that they had revolted, either on their own account or
because they'd been corrupted or co-opted by some
cunning enemy. That kind of insidious maneuver seems
to be typical of the war in which they were engaged
at the time . . . and still are, after a fashion. It wasn't
fought with guns, even at its height; its weapons were
biological: manufactured microbial agents. Since the
revolt, the barrel-boys have been more careful in the

selection and engineering of their biological instruments . . . those that survived the upheaval as well as new ones, especially the minotaurs they release into the labyrinth, many of which are subtle weapons, becoming ever subtler."

"The Germans were rumored to be working with offensive bacterial agents," Tom put in. "They'd already deployed several types of poison gas, and we had our own stockpiles. If the armistice hadn't been signed, we'd probably have seen more and worse by now. It seems to be a logical development of sophisticated warfare."

"Well," Oates said, "I didn't see any such weapons in action, but I got the impression that they were very sophisticated indeed, and that they were, indeed, stockpiled, ever ready for deployment if circumstances warranted. As I said, the Antarcticans' war has been quiet for a long time—a stalemate far more complex and sustained than the one in the trenches of Western Front, to judge by the sketchy descriptions you've given me—but it still produces the occasional skirmish. They don't have big guns, in order to deliver their sneaky weapons in shells, or airplanes to drop them from above, obviously, but they have the labyrinth, and subtle methods of transmission."

Tom deduced from Oates' account that he had not actually met the Antarcticans in the flesh—in the sense that he'd met Janet or Helen—but he had entered into their dreams. That was what had sustained him, dead or alive, and preserved him. They were, of course, still dreaming. It was their dream, rather than the crevasse, that had been the real trap, the actual pitfall, into which he had fallen ... and from which he had eventually been released, or expelled, in the carefully-preserved flesh sustained by the cryonic chill of the Antarctic ice.

Trying to pull the threads of his vision together, Oates seemed almost to fall into another bottomless pit, into a collective dream of life-forms unlike ours, which had been asleep, or maybe dead, for many millions of years. Exactly where or when he had been before he surfaced again in Yorkshire, it was impossible for him to say, perhaps because he had no longer been anywhere or anywhen, but merely *in between*. He'd been outside the flow of material events, but not so far outside that he couldn't look into that flow occasionally. He could see the Other Antarctica, and he could see fragments of our world too, and he had occasionally had the illusion—perhaps even the reality—of walking therein. The Other Antarctica wasn't confined by the geography of our Antarctica, although it was rooted there. The mystery of how he had walked to the entrance to the driveway wasn't really a mystery, even though it was a paradox. He really had, it seemed, *walked* from Antarctica—directly, in the ultimate instance, albeit on legs that were still damaged and enfeebled. The barrel-boys, it seemed, had been in a hurry to send him on his mission, just as they were in a great hurry for him to complete it.

"I've dreamed being back before," he said, vaguely. "I've been to the Transvaal, to London, even to Eton. I thought of the excursions as constitutionals—refortifying visitations of familiarity, you would probably have called them, in your flowery fashion—but I have a sneaking suspicion that the Antarcticans might have been using them to carry out reconnaissance and experiments, making sure of me before entrusting me with the seeds and the mission to grow them."

"And what will happen when the mission is over?" Tom asked him. "For that matter, *when* will it be over? I've already ascertained and demonstrated that the things can be developed, in the right environmental conditions—how far do we have to go?"

"I don't know," the other replied, seemingly annoyed at not knowing.

Presumably, Tom thought, Oates could walk back to the Other Antarctica just as easily as he had arrived—but why would he want to when his mission was complete? Wouldn't he want to move on, to see his family, to begin a new life if the old one couldn't simply be resumed?

He made that suggestion to his guest.

Oates frowned. "I don't know," he repeated, tiresomely—but he had given them no indication of wanting to contact his family, or anyone at all outside Andersley. That was not in the specifications of his mission. Presumably, he would go as mysteriously as he had come, if and when *they* summoned him. One way or another, they were watching him, tapping his dreams; they could order him back at any moment, without even sounding an audible reveille.

Tom was dutiful, now, in keeping Helen up to date, in reporting the meager results of the day's labor He was dutiful, too, in asking Mercy about her day, and hugging her as closely as he dared. He made a point of kissing Helen when he said goodnight to her—but she was not entirely grateful for his efforts. She was particularly disappointed by his impotence to discover how long the nurturing of what she, like Oates, persisted in calling the "vampire starfish" might go on and what might become of them when they were fully grown, and she didn't like the idea that the barrel-boys might be eavesdropping on everyone's dreams.

"Are they responsible for your nightmares?" she wondered aloud one evening, in the study, after Mercy had been sent to bed. Oates had retired to his room as well, ostensibly to read.

"I doubt it," said Tom. "They haven't changed since Oates arrived. I don't dream about the creatures, or anything Oates has told me. If anything, they're probably keeping such matters out of my dreams."

Helen was still unimpressed. "A pity, then," she opined, "that they can't keep other matters out . . . or don't want to."

"Perhaps they find them interesting," Tom suggested. "For them, it's probably a learning experience . . . perhaps an amusement. Either way, though, they must be getting bored by now. Too much repetition."

"According to the story that you and Oates have stitched together," she said, "they're patient, and if they're millions of years old they're obviously not easily bored. But what can they be waiting for? Why is Oates still here?"

"I don't know," was all that Tom could say. "Neither does he. But I must admit that I don't want him to go just yet. It's good to have him here, now that he's his old self again."

"You keep saying that," Helen observed, "but he *isn't* his old self, is he? He might be able to reminisce with you about your time at that dreadful school, and the hellishness of the Boer War, but he can't be his old self, can he? He's been dead and dreaming for seven years. He's no longer even human."

"Yes he is," Tom told her, although he didn't like to contradict her. "He's a trifle chilly to the touch, but he's made of our flesh and blood, nor some kind of Gordian knot."

"If you say so—but Janet isn't convinced, and nor am I. Even if it's true, I wish he weren't here, and that you weren't growing his blessed magic beans. I'd feel a lot safer."

Safer? Tom wanted to say, at the risk of adding contradiction to contradiction. *Were we safe before he came? Safe from the after-effects of the war? From the influenza epidemic? From everything that the world still has in store for us, entirely of its own accord. Nothing is safe now, for us or for Mercy. How can we ever know safety again?* But he didn't say anything. To broach that argument would be conduct unbecoming. It was safer to talk about the hypothetical Antarcticans.

"There's no evidence that we're under any kind of threat," he reminded his wife. "They saved Oates' life, or brought him back to life. His heart is beating, and he isn't so very cold. His old leg-wound has scarred over completely, although he still has the occasional twinge, and you'd never know that his toes had been frostbitten. They didn't bring him back from the dead all at once, but they gave him the means to recover completely.

They might be monsters of a sort—but they seem to be gentle and benevolent monsters. They can't have any reason to wish us ill, and we have no cause for anxiety. We have no idea what's going to happen—but that doesn't seem to me to be a bad situation, after so many years of knowing *exactly* what was bound to happen, sooner or later . . . until the armistice."

Helen conceded that point, as she had to, and Tom gave her a hug, for which she was duly grateful, although she wasn't sure, as yet, that he had come all the way back to life, or that he could.

Privately, however, he was by no means reassured by his own arguments, and he kept probing in his conversations with Oates.

"Accepting, as you say, that the Earth was inhabited before: before our kind of life—the entire ancestral tree connecting monad to man—emerged from the sea," he said, while they worked in the greenhouse, under grim gray daylight of a kind that Tom thought typical of Yorkshire, "are you sure—can you be sure—that the barrel-boys are simply the result of a different evolutionary sequence. You say that there have also been incursions from elsewhere—incursions of star-spawn. Perhaps your Antarcticans, and their enemies, didn't evolve here at all. Perhaps they came from elsewhere, as colonists, and once they'd arrived and established their plantations, as our colonists do, they became involved in fighting colonial wars, as our colonists do. Maybe the entire universe is a battlefield, and Earth is just a remote island, a backwater claimed by three or four different powers, possession of which alternates, like the islands in the Far East, one of many outposts in a great Imperial game. It's possible, isn't it, that our kind of life is actually the only kind *native* to the Earth?"

"It's possible," Oates conceded graciously, "but it's not the impression I get."

Tom couldn't help speculating further, making up his own stories in the same vein as Oates. He was a practical agriculturalist, after all, a son of Cain; he understood colonialism better than the poor hapless planters who only had to do it.

"Perhaps the monads that eventually gave rise to humans did emerge by some strange process of spontaneous chemical evolution from the oceanic slime," he suggested to Oates, "but perhaps not. If the Earth really was colonized by star-spawn in the remotest depths of prehistory, it's surely possible that the primeval oceans were seeded, like a vast *jardin d'acclimation*? The key to the success of the colonial project is feeding the colonists, providing them with an adequate ecological basis, but colonists can't just import seeds from home and expect them to grow in alien conditions; they have to breed them selectively, to produce varieties that thrive in the new conditions, while providing the necessary nutrition and the other things that plants supply to plantation owners: materials for weaving and construction."

"I doubt it," Oates said. "I can't imagine that you're thinking along the right lines."

Your lack of imagination doesn't constitute an argument, Tom thought, *especially as your imagination seems to be subject to a certain amount of censorship, a victim of what the French call Anastasia's scissors.*

148

"It may be nothing you've ever dreamed," he conceded, aloud "and that might make it unlikely... but it's not impossible." After all, he thought, the Antarcticans, according to Oates, were very long-lived and very patient. They had been dormant for a very long time, apparently waiting—but waiting for what? Was it conceivable that they had been waiting for an experiment in acclimation to come to slow maturity, for a crop they had planted in the Earth's oceans thousands of millions of years ago to ripen, for monads to turn into men, and for men to develop... what? Not civilization, probably, and perhaps not anything that humans themselves would consider a significant achievement.

Perhaps, Tom thought, well aware that he was biased, they had been waiting for men to produce *jardins d'acclimation* of their own, to perfect the art of selective plant breeding? Perhaps they had been waiting for the Sons of Cain finally to triumph over the Sons of Abel... except that they did not seem to be Sons of Cain themselves. The test crop that they wanted him to investigate for them seemed to be animal rather than vegetable, if that elementary distinction was still meaningful within the great chain of being built from Gordian knots.

And, he remembered, there was also a complicating factor. The Antarcticans were at war. If they were colonists, they weren't the only colonists. Like the French, the English and the Dutch—and the Germans if they had been able to muscle in on the act—following in the footsteps of the Spanish and the Portuguese, fighting over the Pacific islands, the Americas, India and Africa, their attempts to establish secure and fruitful plantations were being carried out against a backcloth of warfare, albeit subtle warfare fought with agents that were doubtless themselves products of gardens and laboratories, endeavors methodologically akin to those of Banks, Parmentier and Bligh, but infinitely more sophisticated.

The fact that the Antarcticans were a very different kind of life from the elements of the monad/man sequence was a complication of the hypothetical schema, but an intriguing one. They might also be very different from their competitors. Some of *their* enemies, Tom thought, partly on the basis of what Oates had told him, were probably even more different from the monad/man sequence than they were, and the war in which they were engaged might be very different indeed from the kind of trench warfare that had first been employed by the Boers and then had been greatly sophisticated in the recent War.

It was all just speculation—waking dreams—but it was engrossing as well as intriguing. Tom would have liked to be able to discuss it more earnestly with someone—either with Oates or with Helen—but he did not dare. According to Oates, the Antarcticans couldn't read conscious thoughts, but once conscious thoughts became subjects of discussion, they might also be adopted into the substance of dreams. So he followed his flights of fancy alone, in secret, immune from criticism and supplementation.

The basic hypotheses seemed clear enough, in principle: the transplantation of crops, the conquest of new environments, and the science of assertive biology.

Perhaps we, he posited—*by which I mean every life-form known to us and related to us—are just the result of some cosmic project of acclimation, the end-product of seeds sown in the seas of Earth with a view to . . . well, to begin with, to a few billion years of adaptive evolution by natural selection, in order that one day the Earth would be ready . . . that* we'd *be ready . . .*

For what?

Tom dared not put the hypothesis to Oates explicitly, but he felt that he could beat around the bush, in a purely hypothetical manner, that being the best way not to alert his masters. It seemed safe, at least, to raise again the possibility that the barrel-boys had not evolved on Earth, that they might be star-spawn, and that they might regard Earth as a colony of sorts.

Oates agreed again that that was possible, hypothetically—even plausible, given what he knew—but he suggested that Tom's thinking was too anthropocentric.

"They aren't mayflies, Linny," he said, pensively. "They don't work on our kind of timescale. I'd say that they don't think like us if I could imagine any other way of thinking than simply thinking, but . . . well, however they think, and however they dream, they do it in the long term. I don't think you can simply project your way of seeing things—our way of thinking—on to them. I believe that they're stranger than you or I imagine . . . stranger than you or I *can* imagine."

"And yet," Tom mused, "they sent you to me with a mission, in order to use the facilities of Andersley, in order to use my greenhouse, and my expertise as a Son of Cain. There's surely an overlap in our ways of thinking, our purposes." But that chain of thought was too close to the mental line he'd decided to draw, and he thought it politic to continue it in private.

If Earth really is a colony, he thought, *and the barrel-boys are colonists, then our kind of life might be a crop of sorts. On the other hand, many aspects of it might be unintended consequences, more pest than product, an inconvenience or threat to their ultimate objective. Seemingly, it's useful for the moment, here and now, for something, and it might also useful to their competitors, the rival powers, if they also know we're here, and are capable of tapping our dreams. On the other hand, if we're useful in some way to the barrel-boys, it's possible that their adversaries consider us, for that very reason, to be a weed, or a pest. Clearly, the Antarcticans are capable of capturing us and using us, even when we ought to be dead . . . even, perhaps, when we* are *dead . . . at least when they can trap one of us in one of their pitfalls. Their pickings in the Antarctic must be thin, I suppose, if they need something brainier than penguins—but if there's another Arctic, the creatures hiding there might have had a better harvest in the last century or so, human-wise, with Sir John Franklin and all the people who went to look for him and disappeared in his wake. Is there another Arctic, I wonder?*

He asked Oates that question, assuming that it would seem natural enough.

"I don't know, Linny," Oates said. "I never got a glimpse of it, if there is . . . but that doesn't necessarily mean that there isn't."

I'm right about the thin pickings in the Antarctic, though, Tom thought, *and there's no longer any reason for glory-hunters like Scott to go back, now that Amundsen has reached the Pole and Scott's cadaver has been found. How thankful ought I to be for that?*

Tom did not find it a particularly horrible thought that humans, and all the life-forms to which they were related, might simply be weeds in an alien plantation that had run wild while the owners were temporarily indisposed. It would be a blow to human esteem . . . but to how much esteem were the humans who thought of themselves as "advanced" entitled, after Mons and the Somme and all the instruments of death that had been deployed there? Lions led by donkeys perhaps . . . but in the final analysis, all just vermin. He had always argued, in his days as a schoolboy heretic, that humans ought be a good deal prouder of having evolved from a humble monad, by virtue of the marvelous progress they had made since, than if they had sprung arbitrarily and ready-made from the hand of a whimsical Creator . . . but viewed dispassionately, were there any real grounds for pride at all?

He laughed then, silently, at the thought of what the Old Earl—a devout man, in his own eccentric way— might have thought of the proposition that there might really have been a creator who had gone to some trouble to forge humankind, but that it was a barrel-shaped entity with five tentacular feet at one end and a mess of sense-organs at the other, and had only had its own image in mind when designing sea-cucumbers.

In the meantime, Oates had been prompted by Tom's questions to a little speculation of his own.

"I don't believe that the barrel-boys are star-spawn at all," he told Tom. "I think they're native, but simply very different from us. I think the Antarctic really belongs to them, that it's their original homeland. The Other Antarctica might seem horrible to creatures like us, but to them it's native soil, which has changed vastly since the time of their birth, but for which they still feel a profound attachment and affection. The Antarctica in which they're dreaming now isn't the Antarctica of their heyday, and there can only be a few fugitive echoes of that heyday, old and decayed . . . but not entirely dead, and certainly not forgotten. It's peaceful now, neglected, but I think that when they have to defend it, whether against local threats of star-spawn, they're prepared to fight for it to the death, and beyond . . ."

"Perhaps the Arcticans feel the same way," Tom suggested, dryly.

"They can't," Oates said flatly. "There's no land under the Arctic ice-cap except for a few paltry islands. If there are any Arcticans now, they must have come from elsewhere, a long way away."

"Which might not make them feel any less possessive or patriotic," Tom suggested. "Look at the so-called Americans, who were the desperate displaced scum of Europe only half a century ago, but now consider themselves to be the lords of the Earth, custodians of the great American Dream."

"*Americans!*" said Oates, contemptuously. Tom wondered whether the Antarcticans pronounced their word for the Arcticans in the same tone, figuratively speaking.

"But there are other continents," Tom said—aloud, although he was really talking to himself. "Whether there's another Arctic or not, there might be Other Africas, Other Australias, other labyrinths . . ."

"Other Yorkshires?" Oates suggested, a trifle mischievously.

"Perhaps," Tom, agreed, although that suggestion was too close for comfort . . . especially given that Oates' last way-station before limping along the driveway of Andersley had probably been the abandoned coal-pits . . . pits that some of the locals considered to be haunted, and not by the spirit of the Old Earl, whose forefathers had owned them.

"But you don't really have any idea—do you?—of what the Other Antarctica is like," he said to Oates. "To you, it's literally the stuff of dreams, and not your own dreams. You imagine it as mountainous, but the mountains you imagine aren't really mountains, and might be purely symbolic. You see them in your mind's eye as vast and strange, like aspects of the visions that De Quincey describes having had under the influence of opium—and you must, in fact, have been dosed with something akin to opium while you were in the custody of the barrel-boys. Your story, such as you've pieced it together, is surely reminiscent of an opium dream; how else can we conceive your continual references to things 'beyond the Mountains of Madness?' Perhaps the barrel-boys are addicts of some kind of mind-altering drug. That would be understandable; if they've been dreaming for a billion years, especially if they've died in the meantime, they'd be bound to have gone insane, don't you think?"

Oates laughed. "No," he said, "I don't. I don't know what their plan is, but I know that they have one. They're perfectly rational."

But you're their pawn, Tom thought. *You would say that, wouldn't you?*

Personally, he wasn't so sure. His philosophizing suggested that the business with the "seeds," even if it really was a plan, and even if it was a plan by means of which the waddling barrels hoped to obtain some advantage in their mysteriously slow war, might be a crazy plan, like so many made by Haig and the Allied High Command, which had only led to hundreds of thousands of hapless Tommies being mown down by machine-gun fire. It might be the result of twisted monomania, or alien schizophrenia, or just plain old derangement. It was surely a plan of some sort, but that didn't mean that it was a sound plan, for colonial conquest or any lesser purpose. Seeds from beyond the Mountains of Madness might be anything or nothing, maybe harmless by virtue of being doolally tap, but maybe not.

Either way, though, Tom figured that he had to do his best to achieve what Oates had asked of him, for Oates' sake. Even though his dreaming masters hadn't made any dire threats, Oates might well come to grief if he couldn't do what the barrel-boys wanted of him. Even though his heart was beating and his wounds had healed, Oates was still stuck in a dream, or a nightmare, which might well be subject to arbitrary dissolution at a moment's notice. If *they* got what they wanted, there was a chance that they might simply let him go, honoring the tacit bargain they'd made, if they were honest and honorable monsters . . . but there was also a chance, obviously, that they weren't and wouldn't. There was nothing Tom could do, however, if the latter possibility turned out to be the case. He had to play ball and hope.

He did confess to Oates that he was afraid for him.

"I'm worried, given what you've told me," he said, "that the dreamers might stop dreaming you. I'm worried that although they've brought you back to life, they might withdraw that privilege at any moment. If they don't get what they want, they might simply *discard* you."

"Don't worry about that, Linny," he said. "That's a risk I have to take. In any case, that's not what I'm afraid of."

"What *are* you afraid of?" Tom asked, warily. He could easily imagine that there might be an abundance of possible fears available to his friend beyond a mere slippage into delayed oblivion.

Oates just shook his head, and wouldn't say. He was a certified hero, who wasn't given to confessing weaknesses or discussing anxieties, but Tom didn't think that that was the real reason for his reluctance. His guess was that Oates was afraid of what *they* might dream next. He was afraid of what he might have started by falling into their pitfall trap—probably the first intelligent creature to have done so for millions of years, unless penguins were a lot smarter than people imagined. He was afraid of what *they* might do, now that they knew far more about human capabilities, thanks to close examination of his dreams, than they had known before, when they were only able to make vague and distant contact with the human collective unconscious. Tom's guess was that Oates was less afraid of the plan of which the barrel-boys had made him a part than the future plans they might make, on the basis of the success or failure of the experiment in progress.

In a way, Tom supposed, it didn't matter whether his guess was right or wrong. There was nothing he could do about it. But that was a horrible thought in itself. Humans couldn't hold back the ice, if the ice were to come again, for all the Yorkshire stubbornness in the world—and they couldn't hold back the dreams that *they* were dreaming, if those dreams turned to nightmare. If a new Ice Age began—the latest of several—humans civilization could be crushed, ground down to dust, without having any way to fight back.

If the story that Oates had reconstructed had any import at all, it was the lesson that human beings, human intellect and human civilization were utterly trivial in the context of cosmic time and cosmic events. On the world stage, individually and collectively, humans were impotent, in spite of their delusions of grandeur and their nonsensical boast of being made in the image of God.

Even people who believed that they were made in the image of God, Tom thought, only believed it in order to grasp at the hopeful straw that when events overwhelmed them, they might be saved by divine intervention, by a miracle. Tom had never believed in miracles, or in people who claimed to have seen them. He knew that the newspapers had reproduced dozens of accounts claiming that the ghosts of the bowmen of Agincourt, or angels sent directly from Heaven, had helped to cover the retreat from Mons—but he had been at Mons, in the midst of that retreat, and he hadn't seen a single ghostly archer, let alone an angel. His men had been on their own, too busy fleeing disaster even to pray, just as they had four years later on the Chemin des Dames. *Plus ça change, plus cést la même chose.* Tom believed in evolution, in *acclimation*, in human responsibility—but even that was an effort, sometimes, and in the end, he had stopped hoping for any significant historical result therefrom.

On the other hand, he knew, individual humans were not simply victims of history. In their own lives they could achieve personal victories—small victories, but vital to them. That ought not to be beyond his reach. In spite of recent experience, that was a corner he could still turn, if only he could contrive the maneuver. He was a scientist, after all. If he could nurture alien pseudo-ophiuiroids and bring them from embryo to maturity, surely he could repair his broken relationship with his wife, whom he loved and who loved him?

VIII

TOM still had no real idea what to expect of the "pseudo-ophiuroids," even though their development now seemed well advanced in two cases. They were material, seemingly not the stuff of dreams, but there was nothing in their materiality to offer firm indications of their origin and ancestry. Tom had dissected the casualties of the experiment, but had learned nothing more from that operation to add to what his first dissection had taught him. He had almost begun to hope that the two specimens that were still alive but lagging behind their siblings would die, so that he could dissect a more advanced individual, but he dared not contemplate killing one, or trying to. That might be dangerous, in more ways than one.

He recalled, frequently, that Oates had warned him in the very beginning that there might be danger in completing the task that had been allotted to him, but he could see no clue as yet to the direction from which that danger might come. While the pseudo-ophiuroids still remained quiescent, alive but unmoving, they did not seem at all threatening. Nevertheless, he had to remain alert, to monitor them with the utmost care, especially as Oates was becoming visibly more anxious, evidently fearful of some possibility that he could not spell out.

He was not the only one to have observed that. Helen said nothing, but Janet took the liberty of asking him one evening whether Oates was worried about something.

"When he first arrived," the housekeeper said, "he seemed to be sleeping very soundly, in spite of his injuries . . . but now, he has bad dreams." *Like you*, she carefully refrained from adding.

"I know," Tom told her. "He's worried about our experiment, I think."

"Because it's not going well?" Janet queried, cunningly.

"No," Tom said, "because it's nearing its end, and he's becoming impatient to see the result."

"Well," said Janet, "it can't come too soon for me, either. Lady Andersley is anxious too, and the whole house knows it. There's something in the air, Sir, and it isn't just Scotch mist."

"There's nothing for you or the staff to worry about," Tom assured her, blandly. "It's just a biological experiment."

"That's doubtless what Daedalus said about the minotaur, sir," the housekeeper ventured. It could not be an analogy she had picked out of thin air; it had to be based on things overheard, but at least she hadn't raised the subject of vampire starfish.

"Probably not," Tom countered, "but the minotaur didn't do him any harm, and even his wings didn't let him down—only Icarus flew too close to the sun. Legend can be very unfair in its judgments and often gives poor counsel. We'll be fine, Janet . . . there are far worse dangers abroad in the world than the things in my greenhouse. Perhaps that's what Oates has realized, while he's been catching up on the seven years of news he missed."

Janet's anxiety, however, and the fact that she had ventured to express it, did nothing to reduce his own, which was increasing, like an echo of Oates'. Naturally, he continued to take refuge in increasingly venturesome speculation.

Perhaps, he proposed to himself, the pseudo-ophiuroids had been actively produced, by means of biological engineering, by life-forms that had been buried under the Antarctic ice for an unimaginable interval of time—but he rejected that hypothesis immediately. If they had been engineered, they would have been designed, and would not have been designed in such a way that the experiment he was conducting could be necessary. They had to be natural creatures, perhaps creatures that had once been selectively bred with some purpose of acclimation in mind, but nevertheless natural, with corollary inconveniences. Perhaps they had fallen into our familiar world from the mysterious "Other Antarctica," or perhaps they were from another world elsewhere on the cosmic battlefield, but they were surely unlikely to be artificial organisms confected by the barrel-boys. They were made of the same chemical elements as Earthly life, though, and his chemical analyses indicated that their filamental structure was based on exceedingly long chains of carbon atoms, supplemented by hydrogen, nitrogen and so on, like the protein building-blocks of familiar life but chemically distinct therefrom.

Given that basic chemical similarity, Tom thought it likely that the alternative evolution of the Gordian knot creatures would follow a similar pattern to the complexification of the monad/man sequence, adapting to similar environmental circumstances and challenges with similar anatomical inventions. He would not have been surprised, to begin with, to see the "magic beans" behaving like earthly beans, putting forth shoots and roots, to see the shoots turning into stems, and the stems developing branches. When that did not happen, he simply shifted the grounds of his expectation, and anticipated that they would develop like animal larvae, the appearance of pentamerous symmetry suggesting that they would follow a template similar to that of echinoderms.

The two that had grown most rapidly conformed obligingly go that revised expectation. They grew sideways rather than up or down in the bloody mulch, putting out limbs of a sort, with a fundamental pattern that made them resemble starfish, at least a little. It was only when Tom had changed the soil in the pots, or switched them to bigger containers, that he was able see them clearly, in every detail, but he changed the soil every couple of days, carefully, monitoring its depletion and alteration with a view to identifying the nutrients they required and the dosages that facilitated their growth and development. The two that grew seemed to be absorbing various materials at a rapid rate, soaking up the erythrocytes in the ox-blood, and the plasma too.

He replanted the two that did not develop as rapidly several times, trying to give them every chance to catch up, but they did not seem able to take full advantage of the opportunities he gave them. He soon concluded that the deficiency was in the "seeds" rather than the matrix; the bloody soil in which the most successful pair thrived was simply not as effective in enabling their cousins to develop.

"Because they're so similar externally," Tim told Oates, "I don't know whether the one I chose for dissection was one that could have developed rapidly or one of the slower ones; although the two that died might have been casualties of my attempt to grow them hypdroponically, it's also possible that they too were defective. The sample size is too small for me to draw any firm conclusions, but if I had to guess I'd suspect that to be the case. The embryonic process that produces the complex tangles as the subsidiary knots in the filament must sometimes go awry spontaneously."

"Don't worry about it," Oates said. "Two complete successes out of seven is a trifle disappointing, but it's infinitely better than none, and substantially better than one. I'm not dissatisfied."

"Does that mean that the barrel-boys aren't dissatisfied?" Tom asked.

"I think so. You've done a good job, Linny—everything I and they could have expected of you." But Oates did not sound entirely convinced.

"I can't claim any credit for the two that have developed," Tom told him. "It was simply a matter of luck. Anyone could have done as much . . . anyone with a heated greenhouse and access to an abattoir."

"I don't believe that, Linny. You realized very rapidly that their appetite for blood was prodigious, and you've been ingenious in supplementing it with other necessary compounds, organic and inorganic. You didn't delay in making a special arrangement with the slaughterhouse for daily deliveries, or in ascertaining that bovine blood seems to be noticeably more effective than sheep's blood. You determined that they appreciated extra iron as well, as well as strong doses of magnesium and iodine and traces of other substances. Another experimenter wouldn't have done nearly as well, I'm sure."

Tom shook his head. "That was mostly luck as well," he insisted "I hadn't enough time or specimens to attempt fine discriminations with regard to organic supplements or inorganic salts. I was fortunate that my assumption with regard to sea salt panned out, given that they might have had a very different ion balance to maintain, and almost everything else I've fed them is simply stuff that gardeners supply to their earthly crops."

"But you also figured out immediately that manure, peat and other products of decay weren't helping them. You can call it good experimental design if you want, but it seems to me to be more intuitive than that. You're not going to shake my conviction that you have a gift, Linny."

Helen wasn't so complimentary. "It's all very well for you to keep them fed with daily deliveries from the abattoir," she said, "but it's generating some ominous gossip in the village, and if the gossips knew what you were actually doing with the blood the rumors would be even worse. What do these things do for blood in their natural habitat? What can they do, except suck the blood of living animals . . . or humans?"

"If they have a natural habitat," Tom told her, "I'm fairly certain that it doesn't contain any human beings, so creatures like us can't figure among their natural prey. They don't seem to have developed any apparatus for biting or suction, and even if they do develop a system of extraction as they develop further, it doesn't mean that they'd suck their victims dry. Efficient parasites are prudent; they don't kill their prey, because what's good for the creatures they parasitize is good for them; it's in their interests to keep them alive and healthy. If you live on blood, you want to keep the organisms whose blood you drink in the pink."

"Like mosquitoes? Or tsetse flies?" Helen objected.

"Rare exceptions," Tom countered, "crude and primitive—and it's their own parasites that do the damage to humans, while treating the flies discreetly. The organisms I'm nurturing are much more sophisticated than that."

"And that's supposed to reassure me, is it?" Helen went on. "They're vampires, but they'll want to keep us alive in order to maintain their supply of fresh blood, much as we force our cows to calve every year and then take the calves away for slaughter in order that they can keep supplying us with milk from their bloated udders."

She was exaggerating, of course—but it did occur to Tom, in response to her fears, to wonder how such organisms, if they did indeed have a natural habitat, on Earth or elsewhere, could ever have found an environment of blood-soaked fields in which to evolve and thrive. Even the battlefields of France couldn't have sufficed. Ergo, the organisms had probably been deliberately adapted, albeit not specifically designed . . . but for what purpose? That was an uncomfortable train of thought, from the very outset, and he shelved it for the time being.

It was in the third week of their growth that the two survivors began to peep above the surface of the soil—and it seemed to Tom that *peeping* was exactly what they were doing. They didn't have anything that looked like vertebrate eyes, or even insectile compound eyes, but the short stalks that began to protrude from the soil did have black shiny tips that were not entirely unlike the stalked eyes of lobsters. They seemed to be light-sensitive, and they seemed particularly appreciative of the bright electric lighting with which Tom supplemented the weak daylight and prolonged the shortening daylight hours of November—though not as much, he presumed, as they appreciated the effects of the gas-fueled underfloor heating and the humidifiers. One specimen that he briefly placed in cooler circumstances, by way of experiment, almost immediately fell behind its twin, so he stopped that trial and gave both his star pupils as much heat and humidity as he could without prejudicing the health of their Earthly neighbors.

Oates seemed to be a little disappointed with the Earthly neighbors. He didn't altogether disapprove of Tom's careful investigations of pineapples and bread-fruit, but bananas seemed to him to be banal.

"Why bother with bananas, Linny?" he asked. "I mean, there are bananas all over the world. They grow easily, anywhere that's hot, with no difficulty at all, as far as I know."

"They do indeed, Titus," Tom told him. "There are Banana Republics in consequence, offering eloquent testimony to the awesome accomplishments of trans-plantation in the service of colonization. And it's all artifice. Bananas are dioecious: they have separate male and female trees—but only the female trees produce fruit, so they're the only ones of commercial interest. All the banana plantations outside of south-east Asia—and there are, as you say, an enormous number of them, scattered far and wide—consist almost entirely of fe-male trees produced vegetatively, grown from cuttings of cuttings of cuttings; and none of their flowers is ever fertilized. There are only a limited number of male banana trees left in the wild, and they're in danger of extinction, even while their female counterparts go on to ever-increasing triumphs of producing human fod-der—but there's one over there in that corner: perhaps the only one in England, unless there's one at Kew. My harem of female bananas is probably the only popu-lation in the western world that ever gets any sexual satisfaction."

Oates didn't seem particularly interested, any more than Helen had been when Tom had explained it to her. Mercy wasn't old enough yet to have that kind of intimate detail included in explanations—not in Helen's opinion, at any rate. Mercifully, she had never queried Tom's bananas. The brat did, however, ask at dinner one night why Oates always called her father "Linny."

"It was his nickname at school," Oates explained.

"Yes," said Mercy, "but *why?* It's nothing like his real name."

"I carried a key to British *Flora* around whenever I went out on the river, or into the woods," Tom explained, by way of parental duty. "I was learning to identify plants. The other boys called me Linny because it was short for Linnaeus, the man who popularized the classification system of plants used in the *Flora*, although his un-Latinized name was Linné, so it didn't really have to be a contraction. He was a great scientist—primarily a botanist, although he applied his system to the classification of animals as well. His work made it obvious to him that all living species were descended from ancestral species by a process of evolution, all the way back to the primal monad, but he daren't say so, because he would have been silenced and persecuted by religious fanatics. I was proud of the nickname—it seemed far nobler than any of the others with which my contemporaries were afflicted."

"Was Titus a scientist too?" she asked Oates."

"No," he replied. "Titus Oates was a bad priest who invented a fictitious plot and was notoriously condemned, when the lie was exposed, as a disgrace to mankind—but he was the only person known to schoolboys whose surname was Oates, and his first name was distinctive, so it was a natural nickname to give me."

Tom was grateful for that deflection, because it spared him from any possibility of having to explaining that part of the joke of his own nickname was that Linnaeus' classification of plants was based on their sex organs, and that his Etonian comrades were trying to imply, in the tortured and silly way that only schoolboys can, that what he was doing in studying the *Flora* was a kind of pornography. Oates knew better, of course.

Mercy wasn't frightened of Oates, as some of the maids still were, in spite of the improvement in his condition. The fact that Janet and Helen didn't avoid him conspicuously was the result of a sense of obligation, but Mercy genuinely seemed comfortable in his company, and would have sat on his lap if he'd let her. He didn't; it seemed to Tom that Oates was more uncomfortable in the brat's presence than she was in his, not because he didn't like her but because he was anxious that he was not fit company for a child. Helen hadn't tried to hide the sanitarium patients from Mercy while the house had been doing double duty, though, and the child had not only grown accustomed to the proximity of the maimed and the shell-shocked but had joined in, to the extent that she could, with the work of their redemption. She still had the same frame of mind, and Tom suspected that it influenced the way that she treated him as much as it influenced the way she dealt with Oates. He was slightly ashamed of that, thinking that it was not a burden that a father ought not to place on any daughter, let alone one so young.

Helen exhibited a similar inertia, continuing to monitor Oates' wounds, long after it became obvious that they were getting better, continually looking for any sign that the old gunshot wound might be hurting him or that the improvement in his feet might be deceptive.

"He's still cold, though," she mentioned to Tom one night, after Oates had returned to his room to read, as was his habit. "He's completely recovered from the frostbite, which I didn't think possible, but his body temperature is still below normal. Can you explain that?"

"No," Tom admitted, "but it doesn't seem to inconvenience him in any way."

"What about the vampire starfish?" she asked. "Are *they* still cold to the touch?"

"Strangely enough, yes," he said. "Given that the ambient temperature in the greenhouse is so high, I have no idea how they do it, but they do. It's as if they're negatively endothermic, requiring a high external temperature in order to thrive, but maintaining their internal temperature at a level lower than the one at which humans usually functions optimally. Their metabolic cycles are obviously different from ours, but I don't know why they wouldn't have still have the same optimum temperature, given that their biochemistry is still based on long carbon-chains. On the other hand, Oates says that the barrel-boys and other organisms of a similar kind have much longer life-spans than we do, and if that's true of the organisms I'm nurturing, that might be correlated with their lower body temperature." *But not Oates' manifestation of the same phenomenon*, he added, scrupulously, to himself.

"Are the individuals that you have the same sex, or different sexes?" Helen asked, apparently worried that they might start breeding.

"It's impossible to tell," Tom said. "All four of them seem to be anatomically identical, externally, but we don't know as yet whether they might have radical metamorphoses to undergo; the forms we're observing at present might be larval—in which case no sex organs would normally develop until the adult forms appear. Being alien, they might not even have different sexes, or might conceivably have more than two. Even our kind of life only makes limited use of sex, although it's a good shuffler of the Mendelian deck. Advanced organisms capable of vegetative reproduction can do without, as can may micro-organisms . . . but it's unlikely that the organisms I'm observing have no means of producing variations, as the life-system to which they belong, naturally or artificially, is evidently subject to adaptive evolution, albeit on a slow timescale."

"Is there any guess you *do* feel confident making?" Helen demanded, with a hint of exasperation in her voice.

"Not really," Tom admitted, "but I have been toying with a couple of interesting speculations. I've discussed them tentatively with Oates, but he's skeptical."

"Try me instead."

"It seems to me," Tom said, carefully, "that I'm supplying the two that are developing with makeshift incubators. Their appetite for blood suggests to me that their natural habitat, at least in this phase of their existence, might be *inside* some other organism—some quasi-mammalian organism where they can feed directly from its veins."

"Not dinosaurs then?" Helen concluded.

"Too recent," I said, "although it's certainly possible that their blood would have provided sufficient nutrition. The ophiuroids' original host species, if they really are naturally parasitic, is probably something we've never seen, even in fossil form. Fossils are mortal, and entire strata of the crust can be eroded away or pulverized, in the right catastrophic circumstances. If the Earth really is billions of years old, as Oates alleges, there might have been time for more than one evolutionary process to occur on the planet and to be subsequently obliterated—and if it really has been an object of colonization for more than one extraterrestrial species, that widens the range of potential original hosts considerably."

"Do you still doubt what Oates says because you think he might be mistaken, or because you think he might be lying?" she asked, picking up on the covert implication of the "reallys." Her tone was a trifle sharp. If Tom did think that Oates was mistaken or lying, she thought that he ought to have warned her.

"Neither," Tom told her, "but I don't know how much faith one can place in tales told in dreams. Something certainly saved him, or preserved him, in Antarctica—something with abilities we can hardly imagine—but that doesn't mean that it's a reliable informant."

"How are *your* dreams?" she asked, not sharply at all. She knew that Tom's nightmares had not disappeared completely—enough evidence of that was audible through the bedroom wall—but she was evidently wondering whether their substance had altered since she had issued her provocation.

"I don't think there's been any measurable change during the last few days," Tom admitted, reluctantly, "but I haven't been keeping a scrupulous log, so I can't be absolutely sure that the frequency of the dreams isn't decreasing slowly. They're still too frequent and too violent for my liking. I could almost wish that Oates' mysterious manipulator, whatever it might be, would reach into my dreams and provide me with some kind of cosmic perspective: some slow and monstrous consciousness of universal being—anything but the Front: the mud, the bullets, the shells, the tanks, and the gas."

Objectively speaking, Tom supposed, that combination of threats might be the lesser of the evils now on the menu of the imagination, and the lesser of the horrors too, but they were the ones that were saturating his soul. Mercy hadn't said anything about having bad dreams, though, and nor had Helen. Whatever state Oates was in, it didn't seem to be contagious. Oates did admit that the "Other Antarctica" was still present in his head, in some mysterious fashion, while he was awake as well as in his sleep, but he didn't complain about it. He was glad not to be entirely dead, and he wasn't the kind of man who could be terrified by the mere thought of human insignificance in a vast and hostile universe.

By the end of the third week, the surviving creatures had begun to move bodily as well as wiggling their "eye-stalks." They didn't move fast or far, but they did move. At the very least, they squirmed, as if testing their five limbs. They didn't seem to Tom to be at all menacing, even when he imagined them dragging themselves out of the mulch and walking away, like five-legged spiders balanced on the tips of their "feet." Indeed, they seem to him to be rather frail, unready to suffer any reduction in their daily feast of blood, let alone to suffer the English weather, which had grown markedly colder since the relatively mild day on which Oates had arrived.

If they showed any sign at all of becoming danger-ous, Tom sometimes thought, all he would have to do was turn off the gas and leave the greenhouse, taking care to seal the padlock on the door, and they would probably be rendered helpless. At other times, though, that seemed unduly optimistic. Simply because they had required the warmth of the tropical house to trigger their development, and supplies of fresh blood to stim-ulate it, it did not mean that they would immediately be rendered helpless if deprived of those conditions. They had evidently been sent to Tom, and to the special conditions that he could provide, in order to break out of their dormancy, but now that they were active and motile, it might not be simple or easy to plunge them back into inertia.

The more the pseudo-ophiuroids moved, the lon-ger their "legs" became. Tom had already put them into bigger pots twice in weeks one and two, but by the end of week three he was obliged to make use of much larger vessels, more like troughs than pots, and he had to move some of the young potted fruit-trees in consequence, crowding them together more closely than was desirable. If that went on, he thought, it might eventually disrupt his experiments with the fruit trees considerably, the normal progress of which required careful cross-pollination endeavors and the extensive planting out of large numbers of the resultant seeds.

As the "legs" of the "starfish" got longer, the "feet" were physically modified, but not into something bearing a closer resemblance to any kind of animal feet, or cephalopod tentacles. The tips became soft, and were covered in delicate hairs, like a cat's whiskers. *Better that than a scorpion's sting*, Tom thought at first; the hairs seemed to him to be more akin to delicate sensory apparatus, but he could not rule out the hypothesis that they might develop into some kind of blood-sucking apparatus that could facilitate their parasitism, by permitting them to take blood from large living organisms trapped by the grip of the flexible "legs."

"They don't resemble your barrel-shaped entities, except for the basic pentamerous symmetry, do they?" Tom suggested to Oates. "Have you seen anything resembling them in your dreams of the Other Antarctica?"

"I don't recall anything similar," Oates admitted, unhelpfully.

"Might they be minotaurs?" Tom asked, following Oates' example in applying that label to refer to creatures of the labyrinth in general.

"Perhaps," he said. "Yes, they might be . . . but the creatures I initially invented that nickname to describe were dangerous. I never saw any, so I can't say for sure that none of them look like these, but . . . these don't seem to me to be hostile at all. They seem to me to be rather . . . beautiful."

"I don't think Helen would agree with you," Tom said. "Quite the reverse, in fact. In spite of only having five limbs, and moving so slowly, they'd be bound to seem a little *spidery* to her, and thus inherently repulsive. They don't have that effect on you?"

"Not at all," said Oates. "I like them."

"You mean that you can sense the liking that the barrel-boys have for them?" Tom suggested.

"No," Oates replied. "I don't think the barrel-boys have an emotion similar to our . . . esthetic appreciation . . . but I could be wrong."

"Perhaps you haven't seen them, even in your dreams," Tom mused, dredging up the speculative hypothesis that he'd mentioned to Helen, "because they're normally invisible to everyday vision—endoparasitic or endosymbiotic. Their need to bathe in blood suggests to me that their original natural habitat might have been inside a larger organism . . . a much larger organism."

"You think they might live naturally *inside* the barrel-boys?" Oates queried.

"The possibility had occurred to me."

"And you think that once they're mature, the barrel-boys might come to collect them?"

"No. If they are endoparasites, the barrel-boys are more likely to have sent them to be developed here in order to keep them at a distance . . . or possibly to provide them with potential new hosts."

"Us, you mean?" said Oates.

"Unlikely. If they can live on ox-blood, they could probably live on ours . . . but cattle seem to me to be more likely potential hosts. It seems unlikely, though, that they could have evolved as parasites of any organism of our kind, unless they're far less ancient than you believe the barrel-boys to be. They're already inconveniently big to live inside anything smaller than an elephant. Human bodies can accommodate some large endoparasites—guinea worms and some kinds of tapeworms—but they grow within them from tiny beginnings and cease to thrive when they get too big. No, if these things are naturally endoparasitic, it seems to me that their original hosts must have been much bigger than humans, or cows . . . probably even bigger than elephants. Nothing that was ever native to Yorkshire."

Oates did not seem convinced. "You mentioned another word: endosymbiotic. What does that mean?"

"It's an extrapolation of *symbiosis*, which was coined fifty years ago—by the mycologist Heinrich de Bary, I think—to refer to two organisms living closely together in a mutually beneficial fashion. The text-book examples of endosymbiosis include nitrogen-fixing bacteria living inside the roots of plants, and algae living inside reef-building corals. All the familiar examples are single-celled organisms living within multicelled organisms, but there's nothing, in principle to rule out the possibility of multicellular endosymbionts . . . and these creatures aren't cellular at all, so different rules apply, and very different relationships might be possible. The processes by which organisms of our kind evolve and the processes by which filamental organisms evolve might be markedly different. Instead of evolving by mutation and selection, organisms of this alien kind might be capable of evolving by fusion and supplementation . . . but that's pure hypothesis, and very fanciful."

"But if that's the case . . ." Oates said—and then stopped.

Is that his internal censor again? Tom wondered. *Do the barrel-boys want to shut down that bizarre train of thought? Or has Oates simply become tangled in his own train of thought, requiring further thought to analyze the possibilities?*

Tom waited, but all Oates said, in the end, was: "Now that they're mobile, will we be able to keep them in here? Might they escape?"

"Why would they want to escape?" Tom said. "Surely they like it here, where it's warm, and where the blood supply is abundant. The possibility that the organisms' needs might change, that they might be capable of a metabolic metamorphosis, has already been raised, but the question remains: if they were to get out, what would they be looking for? What could they have come here to do that would involve them moving on?" As was his habit, he was not really asking Oates for enlightenment, merely thinking aloud.

"You're right," Oates said. "Whatever they need and want, it's likely to be here . . . but we ought to continue locking the door, to keep them in and to keep others out."

"I always put the padlock on when we leave," Tom reminded him, "and I usually remember to lock the door from the inside when we're working, only unlocking it to accept deliveries." As he spoke, however, he looked up at the glass panes arching over head, and wondered how secure they were. The greenhouse had been built to resist wind and rain but an abrupt impact might shatter the glass. The vampire starfish did not give the impression of being able to deliver such an impact with sufficient force, but their capabilities were untested as yet.

"Perhaps it might be a good idea to send Helen and Mercy away for a few days," Oates suggested, "while we see how things develop."

"No," said Tom, flatly, "it wouldn't."

Oates didn't ask him why not, thus sparing him the embarrassment of evading the question awkwardly—the answer to which was that if he sent Helen away, no matter what reason he gave, she might well take the opportunity not to come back, giving up on their wounded relationship, which was only showing the feeblest signs of healing in spite of the efforts he had promised to make.

In order to change the subject, Tom said: "You've mentioned the barrel-boys having had slave races in their heyday, and domesticated animals, and you implied that they included bulky creatures of more than one sort. Is it possible that those domestic animals were the original hosts of the creatures we've nurtured, or the natural symbionts?"

"Yes," Oates said, after a pause for cogitation, "I suppose that it is, in theory—but I don't think so. I don't believe that you're thinking along the right lines at all."

"What lines should I be thinking along, then?" Tom retorted, a trifle resentfully, feeling that his expertise was being called into question.

"I wish I knew," said Oates. "There was something else you said . . . but it's all so confused. I can't quite see . . . I'm no scholar, Linny, as you know. All this is utterly strange to me. I'm no biologist. I can't see the possibilities the way you can, and I can't think the way you can, always looking for puzzles and paradoxes . . . even stuff you first told me at school, like Sons of Cain and Sons of Abel and all that sort of thing. You'll have to forgive me. I'm relying on you to work it out, Linny. I can't. I try, but I can't."

Tom put his hand on his friend's shoulder. "It's all right, Titus," he said. "I can't make head nor tail of it myself yet—but between the two of us, we'll work it out eventually. Don't try to follow all my abstruse jargon, just stick to your common sense—keep my flights of fancy grounded. It's time to go to dinner anyhow. We have fish, I think, turbot freshly landed this morning at Grimsby. It's said to be good for the brain."

He tried to smile, but couldn't quite manage it. He was rattled, as if something had been disturbed in his perpetual dream, intruding a hint of nightmare into its customary serenity. In spite of what Oates had semi-articulated about "something else he had said," Tom couldn't believe that it was anything in his speculations that had made Oates uneasy. Nor did he think that it was the peeping pseudo-ophiuroids, in whose presence Oates seemed quite comfortable—considerably more so than Tom, who was sure in his own mind that the creatures really did have eyes of a sort, and really were *peeping*, gradually learning to see. It was something else.

"Come on, Titus," Tom said, unbolting the door. "Better get back to the house. The weather is going to turn, if I'm not mistaken. Those clouds look filthy, and they're heading our way."

Oates didn't seem to be listening, although he was looking through the windows of the north side of the greenhouse, in the direction of the massing clouds. For some time—ever since Oates' arrival—the weather had been relatively calm. The prevailing winds in northern England blew from the west, and Yorkshire was shadowed from the worst of the Atlantic weather fronts by the Pennines; by the time the rain-clouds reached the wolds they were usually tamed—but when a considerable low-pressure area had passed to the south, borne by the jet stream, the winds on its trailing edge swung round to blow from the north-east, sometimes bringing blasts of cold air all the way from the Arctic.

Dusk was only just falling, so Tom hadn't switched on the electric lights in the greenhouse, and the gray sky seemed very leaden. When Tom stepped outside, the wind-chill was palpable, and he turned up the collar of his jacket.

"Don't worry, Titus," he said. "Janet will have ordered the fires lit in the dining room and the bedrooms. These precursors of winter happen almost every year; she's well used to them.

Oates was still inside the greenhouse, looking upwards. "Is that snow?" he asked.

Tom stepped back inside and looked up, squinting at the glass. The reason why Oates was uncertain was that the flakes were melting as soon as they hit the warm glass, and then fusing into thin trickles of water. The glass was a poor conductor of heat, though, so Tom knew that the outer surface wouldn't take long to cool down, if snow or sleet fell upon it any volume.

"It's nothing," Tom said. "Just flurries drifting in on the north-east wind. You can hardly feel it outside, in the shadow of the greenhouse. We don't get serious snow in Yorkshire until December, at the earliest, and often not until the end of January. *Then* you might see a serious blizzard—but still trivial by comparison with the Antarctic, I assume. In January and February we sometimes get snowed in, when the snow drifts, the roads get blocked and life grinds to a standstill, but this won't inconvenience us, even if a few inches fall and accumulate temporarily. The blood supplies from the abattoir will still get through . . . but I can lodge a few sheep in the old stables, just in case, if you want to take extra precautions . . . the Old Earl used to do that back in the day, when he anticipated a white-out."

"I don't think I'll be here in January," Oates said, absent mindedly, still looking upwards. It was the first time he had given any indication of expecting his sojourn to come to an end.

"Why not?" Tom asked. "Do you think that Tweedledum and Tweedledee are almost fully-grown, or that they're about to do something spectacular?"

"It's too soon," he said, anxiously. "They're not ready."

"Ready for what?"

"I don't know," he said. "I just have a feeling." He didn't say it the way Helen might have said it, though. He said it like a man who knew that his feelings meant something: that they were premonitions of some kind.

"A *bad* feeling?" Tom queried

"Just a feeling," Oates said—but he added: "You know, don't you, Tom, that I couldn't mean you any harm . . . or Helen, or Mercy? That I'd die defending you, if I had to."

Tom felt a new chill, which wasn't that of the wind. "Do you think you might have to?" he asked.

"I don't know," Oates repeated, for what felt like the thousandth time. "That is, I don't think so. The barrel-boys have nothing against you, and every reason to protect you, if they can. At worst, you're just innocent by-standers. But I have a feeling. That *is* snow, you know—and not just a flurry."

Tom stepped outside the greenhouse again, and looked up. Oates was right. As the clouds thickened overhead, it was beginning to snow. The flakes were tiny as yet, and sparse, but they were getting thicker by the minute. The wind was blowing from the north-east, by no means a gale but insistent, cold air streaming all the way from the ice-cap, picking up moisture over the North Sea.

"It won't last," Tom assured his friend. "It's only November; we're still nearly a month short of the solstice. It might bring back a few uncomfortable memories, but it can only be a subtle reminder. The Antarctic must have been worse by several orders of magnitude."

"It was," Oates replied, "but the snow had been settling there for millions of years, layer upon compacted layer. The ancient snow was long buried, turned into mountains of ice, glaciers as still and solid as glass . . . the turbot sounds good, Linny. Let's go. The star-spawn will be safe, snug and warm here, won't they?"

As he spoke he stepped outside and closed the door, and then stood aside so that Tom could seal the padlock.

"Star-spawn?" Tom queried. "Did you mean to say *starfish*, or do you actually mean that these things are extraterrestrial?"

Even in the deepening gloom, Tom could see Oates' brow furrowing, as if he were trying to ask himself that question, but could not find an answer. All he said in reply was: "Hurry up and get inside, Linny. We don't want you catching cold, do we? You're not used to this kind of thing."

Me? Tom thought. *Not used to snow? This is Yorkshire, not the Transvaal. In the old days, I saw snow every year. Even in France, it got damnably cold in winter.* All that he said aloud, however, as he headed for the house, was: "They say that Lapps and Greenlanders have a dozen different words for snow, because they live with it all the time, and learn to distinguish many different types and aspects. How many terms do your barrel-boys have, do you think?"

"*Greenlanders!*" Oates repeated, in much the same tone as he'd earlier said *Americans!* "Only a dozen?

Typical of nomads, seal-hunting barbarians. They have no idea—no idea at all."

No idea of what? Tom wondered, as he went into the house, let Oates through the doorway, and closed the door again hastily, in order to minimize the loss of domestic warmth. Of what Antarctic snows were like? But surely, no matter how many words they had for it, snow was just frozen water, gathered into pretty little hexagonal prisms, of which it was said that no two were identical, although that was surely implausible. Even on the worlds of other stars, snow could hardly be different; the elementary laws of crystal formation surely would not allow the formation of pentagonal or heptagonal prisms. The Arctic, he knew, was just ice sitting on top of water, save for a few islands. But that didn't mean that there mightn't be Another Greenland, echoing ancient Hyperborea or Ultima Thule, with dreaming Arcticans fighting slow, weird wars against their enemies. Was it conceivable that Arctic snow was somehow different from Antarctic snow, that the Antarcticans and the Arcticans would have a dozen different names for each?

Tom laughed at his own whimsy. The snow that was falling outside was familiar. It was unusual, for November, but not unprecedented, and surely not *wrong*—not, at least, according to *his* vague feeling.

When they went into the study to await the dinner gong, Oates went straight to the north-facing window, the curtains of which had not been drawn. He was peering out into the snow, uncertainly.

"Don't worry," Tom said. "The pseudo-ophiuroids won't get frostbite—or the bananas and pineapples, for that matter. They're as safe in the greenhouse as we are in here—and much warmer, given that Janet hasn't told Maggie to light the fire yet."

"I haven't seen snow for a long time," Oates said.

The remark seemed momentarily bizarre to Tom, but caused him to wonder whether it might, in fact, simply be true. Seven years had passed since Oates had walked out of Scott's tent into the blizzard and fallen into a pitfall trap. His dreams had apparently taken him into a labyrinth, from which he'd obtained glimpses of another Antarctica, which recalled the Antarctica of thousands of millions of years ago. Perhaps, Tom thought, it never snowed in that Other Antarctica. Perhaps, on the other hand, the barrel-boys were simply too familiar with snow to bother to dream it. Oates certainly seemed to be puzzled by this particular snow, reaching out with the palm of his right hand as if to catch the flakes that were falling outside the window, but unable to grasp them because the pane was in the way. Even so, he lifted his hand up toward his eyes, as if in order to inspect imaginary crystals.

"There's nothing to be afraid of," Oates said, clearly addressing himself rather than Tom. "They're perfectly safe, warm and snug. *They* have no way of knowing that we're here, and they can't control the weather." His tone suggested that there was more optimism than conviction in the last sentence.

"Which *they* are you talking about, Titus?" Tom asked. "Not the barrel-boys, I assume?"

Oates laughed. "We only have one word for snow, Linny, and only one word for *them*, which is hardly a word at all, embracing everything that isn't *us*—and very uncertainly, even at that. Ours is a direly impoverished language. Even our discrimination of dream and nightmare is elementary, and stupid. There's so much we can't talk about, Tom."

You can say that again, Tom thought, bitterly.

"And there's so much we can't see," Oates went on, in what Tom, in his impoverished language, thought of as his *waking dream voice*. "We need words even in order to see, you know—and hands too. We need them to conceptualize what we see, and to do that we need to correlate our visual impressions with our knowledge, and with our tactile sensations. The star-spawn see things very differently . . . but they have to learn to see, just as we do, and it isn't easy, for their orphans."

"I suppose the greenhouse is a rather limited and eccentric environment," Tom observed, by way of a subtle prompt.

"The greenhouse is fine," Oates assured him. "Warm, damp, full of lovely fruit-trees . . . not a bad crib, as cribs go. Even the troughs . . . *away in a manger*, as the hymn has it. It keeps out the wind . . . but the glass also walls off the labyrinth. You don't know because you can't see . . . and the star-spawn can't see either, yet. They're immature. That's probably all right, for now . . . but not forever. It's too soon, as yet . . . too soon."

"Because they're still immature?" Tom queried. "Because they have yet to reach . . . puberty?"

That caught Oates' wandering attention.

"Children grow up faster nowadays," he remarked. "It's an effect of war. Look at Mercy."

"No," said Tom, flatly. "Don't look at Mercy. She has ten years in hand of puberty." But he knew what Oates meant. Mercy wasn't wise beyond her years, by any means, but in her view of the world and her knowledge of its horrors she was well in advance of her chronological age. She had seen and felt the effects of the war. She knew what kinds of human injuries were possible, visible and invisible. When she eventually did reach puberty, she would already have lost one kind of innocence. Would that help her to be any wiser? Perhaps.

"Mercy will love the snow, though," he observed. "Children do, don't they? She doesn't seem to mind the cold. But she didn't build any snowmen when the snow accumulated last January. She just liked making snowballs and throwing them. I blame that damned American, myself, who gave her his baseball when he was shipped home."

"*Americans!*" said Oates, with an asperity that Tom could not explain, given that Oates had never been to America, and could not have encountered any of the American soldiers sent to Europe to tidy up the debris of the War.

Returning to the more important point, Tom said: "So you think the pseudo-ophiuroids are still immature—that any sexual characteristics they might be due to exhibit haven't developed yet? So we can't tell, as yet, whether the four of them that are still alive are the same sex, or different sexes?"

Oates shook his head. "Our fellows are all the same," he said, as if that were somehow a tragedy, "and all the more precious for it. You know how it is, Linny . . . except that you don't know that you know. Pray to God that you don't find out . . . that the snow isn't the wrong sort."

"I can't pray to God," Tom reminded him, somewhat at a loss to follow Oates' ramblings. "I'm an atheist, remember, an evolutionist through and through."

"Pray to Saint Linnaeus, then," said Oates. "As patrons go, he's far from being the worst. Imagine if you had no one to turn to for spiritual guidance than Saint Titus, the schemer and perjurer, the disgrace to humankind, according to Judge Jeffreys—who was surely in a position to judge, if it really does take one know one."

"There's no need to pray at all," Tom told him, "and no earthly point in doing it."

"Amen," said Oates, as the dinner gong in the hallway rang.

If the organisms do develop new appetites when they reach their maturity, Tom thought, *it might take their minds off blood . . . assuming that they'll develop minds as well as appetites. Maybe they'll be able to put larval things behind them. Let's hope so; if we get snowed in, the abattoir won't be able to make deliveries any more. Perhaps I ought to convert the old stables into a temporary sheep-fold, as the prudent Old Earl used to do. That way, Oates and I wouldn't be in the firing line if the addicts start suffering from withdrawal and start eyeing us with their beady black blobs, which are only just beginning to discriminate, getting ready to see.*

He cursed himself, though, as he took his seat in the dining room, after nodding politely to Helen and smiling mechanically at Mercy. He knew that he was concentrating his thoughts on the wrong possibilities and that he ought to be trying to assess the significance of the remark that the pseudo-ophiuroids were "all the same" and that their similarity seemed unfortunate to Oates' dream-semi-consciousness.

What is it that I know but don't know that I know? Tom thought—but there seemed to be far too many possibilities in that direction. He hardly knew himself any longer. He was still the same man that he had been before, but he had lost touch with himself somehow. Not a single German bullet had struck him on the Chemin des Dames, but he had left something other than his blood there: some mysterious fragment of what Yorkshiremen, in their sadly depleted language, called the soul—a word he hated because of its ridiculous religious connotations.

The soup was notionally leek and potato, although it was probably mostly turnip and swede, as it usually was when it wasn't oxtail or mock turtle—which it usually wasn't, because bullocks' tails and calves' brains were in short supply nowadays, even though there was an abattoir on the estate whose blood could be commandeered for private purposes instead of going to make black pudding.

"It's snowing harder," Helen commented, in order to make conversation. "It'll settle, now that night's falling. We'll have a carpet a couple of inches thick in the morning."

"Isn't it marvelous?" Mercy put in. "And it's still ages till Christmas."

Oates was still looking at the window, frowning.

"Does the snow bring back bad memories, Captain Oates?" Helen asked, perhaps genuinely curious.

"Don't worry about me, Lady Andersley," Oates said. "I can cope with bad memories."

"And bad dreams?" Helen added presumably aiming a side-swipe at Tom.

"If necessary," Oates confirmed, "but my dreams really aren't that bad. I've never been under bombardment, or forced to charge into a hail of machine-gun fire." That was atypical of him, and Tom judged that he was under stress, in spite of his attempt to manifest and maintain an appropriate dinner-table calm.

"Like Daddy, you mean?" Mercy put in, demonstrating the fact that she might be knowledgeable beyond her years, but still far from wise.

"Eat your soup, darling," Helen commanded, sternly, but stopped short of issuing an explicit order to shut up.

"It's all right," said Tom, making an effort. "Yes, Mercy, I do still dream about the bombardments, and the rattle of the machine guns. But it will fade away, in time."

He was trying to close the discussion down, but in Mercy's mind he was opening it up. "Is that why you no longer keep your revolver in your bedside drawer?" she asked.

It was pointless asking how Mercy knew that he had once kept a gun in his bedside cabinet, or how she knew that it was no longer there. She was a curious child, too often at a loose end.

"I moved it to a safer place," Tom said, calmly. "You mother, quite rightly, didn't approve of my keeping it in the house, even somewhere that you should never have been able to find it."

Mercy didn't apologize. "Is it in the greenhouse?" she asked. She hadn't been in the greenhouse since Oates had arrived, so she didn't know.

"It's in a safe place," he said, thinking that Helen would probably prefer that to a simple yes.

"Eat your soup, darling," Helen repeated, with an emphasis that left no doubt that it was a formal command.

"I'm sorry, Lady Andersley," Oates said. "It's entirely my fault. Inappropriate topic for table conversation."

"It's not your fault at all," said Helen, a trifle sarcastically. "You don't have many ready topics of conversation that aren't . . . but I appreciate the effort you make."

Tom wondered whether that was another subtle side-swipe at him.

The turbot was served, providing an excuse to let conversation lapse. The flesh of the fish was delicate, but it was necessary to concentrate while eating it in order to be on the lookout for stray bones. Mercy's, however, had been carefully chopped up to make sure that there were no bones left in it.

"Are we going to get snowed in?" she asked.

"No, lovely," said Tom. "Even if it settles overnight, it'll melt tomorrow when the wind changes. It's nothing to worry about. Even if the snow did persist and drifted deeply, there'd be nothing to worry about. We have enough supplies laid in, in spite of all the shortages, to keep the house warm and the staff fed. We don't have as many horses now as we had before the war, but I'd still be able to ride to the village if need be. There's nothing to worry about."

Mercy had not asked the question because she was worried, so she accepted Tom's assurances with perfect equanimity, but Oates did not seem convinced, and nor did Helen. Tom found that he had even talked himself into a new anxiety. The curtains had not been closed, and he could see that the snow was coming down thicker and faster now.

"Can I go out to play in the snow after dinner, Daddy?" Mercy asked, although she must have known perfectly well what the answer would be.

"No, lovely," Tom said. "It's already too dark. You can play out tomorrow morning, if the snow hasn't melted overnight. You can build a snowman then, if you like."

Mercy's expression suggested that building a snowman had not been the project uppermost in her thoughts. She accepted Tom's judgment meekly enough, though, doubtless counting the promise as a tactical gain.

IX

A S the dinner progressed to the dessert—treacle pudding with milky custard—it was obvious to Tom that something was the matter with Oates. He was preoccupied and anxious, to the point that Helen asked him whether his legs had begun to trouble him again, and whether he would like a glass of cordial.

"Oh, not at all, Lady Andersley," he assured her. "I feel fine. It's just that the snow reminds me . . ."

He paused.

"Of the South Pole?" Helen prompted, gently.

"Yes," he said—but Tom, who thought he still knew him well, even though he hadn't seen him for the best part of a decade, was sure that he was lying. He must have feared that the deception was transparent, because he felt obliged to supplement it. "It's not so much Scott's tent," he said, "although it wasn't a happy environment. It was the disappointment of getting to the Pole, only to find Amundsen's flag there. To have gone through all that . . . the pain, the weariness, the anger . . . and then to fail . . . To fail because we'd chosen the wrong route, with the wrong equipment, whereas

Amundsen had succeeded because he had relevant experience, and intelligence that Scott lacked. It was a blow . . . a bad blow . . . a fatal blow . . . even if we hadn't . . . if I hadn't . . ."

"I understand," said Helen, cutting him off. "I shouldn't have said anything. I don't know what wrong with me tonight."

Tom judged, though, that the edge in her voice wasn't mere remorse at having said the wrong thing. She knew that Oates was lying—or, at least, dodging the real issue.

Mercy didn't; she took what Oates had said at face value. "They all felt like that," she observed, reflectively.

"All of whom?" Oates asked.

"The wounded soldiers. They all felt like that. Even when they were told that we'd won the war, it didn't make any difference. They all still felt the same . . . that they'd failed. It wasn't the eyes, the arms or the legs they'd lost that hurt them the worst. They were . . ." She stopped, not because she thought she had said too much, but because she didn't have the words necessary to carry on. She had an excuse for that; she was only seven years old.

What's mine? Tom thought, and suspected that Helen was thinking the same thing.

The coffee was terrible. They didn't linger over it. Helen went up to Mercy's room with her, evidently thinking that there was work to be done there, for which simply reading an episode of *Alice in Wonderland* wouldn't suffice.

Tom took Oates into the study, where a fire had been lit during dinner, and poured them both a generous tot of rum, the brandy having run out.

"What's the matter, Titus?" he asked. "I understand, you know, how trivial things can trigger a bad reaction. Figurative grenades go off inside my head sometimes if I hear a distant motor-bike with a rust-hole in its silencer making its way along the road to Driffield. I could understand it, if the snowfall were taking you back, psychologically, to the terrible days before you sacrificed yourself in order to give Scott, Bowers and Wilson a chance, but it isn't that, is it, any more than it's the memory of the sight of Amundsen's flag? It's something to do with the . . . star-spawn?

Oates didn't meet Tom's gaze. He shook his head and took a swig of rum.

"They're not ready," he whispered.

"For what, Titus? For marriage?" He said it lightly, but it wasn't a joke.

Oates looked up at that, and almost laughed, but he also knew that it wasn't a joke, and his laughter wasn't a denial of the relevance of the question.

"For war," he said.

Tom took a deep breath. "How much danger are we in, Titus?" he said. "The truth, please. *How much danger are we in?*"

"You shouldn't be in any danger," Oates said, stubbornly. "You're an innocent bystander . . . you're all innocent bystanders. It wasn't supposed to work out like this, but even so . . ."

Tom assumed that the "all" in question included Helen, Mercy and Janet, and the other household staff. The assurance did not help in the least. He had been in the War. He knew perfectly well that fighting troops did not target innocent bystanders, that all the lurid press stories about German soldiers bayoneting babies and slaughtering old women were simply black propaganda. But he also knew that the trenches in France cut straight through farmland dotted with villages, whose residents, even if they were only tenants and not owners, clung to their homes and the land even when the Front was within spitting distance, and that when the Front collapsed, as it had on the Chemin des Dames, and the troops retreated in disorder, pursued and harassed by tanks and riflemen, the innocent bystanders couldn't get out of the way. Nobody tried to skewer babies with bayonets, but that didn't prevent the babies from dying. It simply couldn't be stopped, if they got caught in the crossfire.

"How much danger are we in, Titus?" he repeated, doggedly.

"None, if I can possibly help it," Oates said. "But . . . I might not be able to. You need to remember that I'm dead, Linny. That revolver in the greenhouse won't do you any good, even if you blow my brains out. You don't understand what you're dealing with."

"But according to you, I could," said Tom. "I just don't know what it is I know."

"It wouldn't help you if you did," Oates insisted, "but whatever happens, Linny, whatever you see and whatever you think, trust me on one point: I will *never* allow any harm to come to Mercy, or to Helen."

Tom took the inference from that that Oates might not be able to stop harm coming to *him*, if he happened to be in the wrong place at the wrong time . . . and that the greenhouse might well qualify as the wrong place, and that tomorrow might easily be the wrong time.

Oates finally looked up and met Tom's anxious gaze. Tom could see the concern in his old friend's eyes, and he knew that Oates was telling him the truth—but there was also something else there: an uncertainty, a kind of blur, as if Oates, no matter how completely he was his old self, was aware of a limitation of that self, aware that he was not only in labyrinthine contact with something that could censor his speech, and perhaps his thought, but something that could, if the necessity arose, take fuller possession of him. He would resist, of course, but he had no reliable idea how effective that resistance might be, just as he had no reliable idea why his saviors had brought him back from the dead and commissioned him to oversee the development of the precious seeds.

The study door opened then and Helen came in, evidently having put Mercy to bed—or tried to—and having questions to ask. Both men turned to look at her. She stared at Oates, inquisitively

Oates shivered, and looked back at Tom, with a gaze that was suddenly frightened. Tom shivered too. He knew that his friend's eyes didn't always see what his own eyes saw, that they sometimes looked into another world that was too strange for him to be able to describe it. At present, while he was looking fearfully at Tom, trying to reassure him of his amity, his urgent sense of responsibility, he was also looking beyond Tom. Something was definitely wrong—but not something *here*, at Andersley: something *there*, in the labyrinth. Something was wrong in the dream of which he was somehow a part, the plan that he was following, in which Tom was a pawn. His saviors were involved in a war, albeit a slow and dormant war, and they had not saved him out of altruism, but because he had the potential, somehow, to be an agent in that war, to make some tiny contribution to its furtherance, to the balance of its long stalemate.

It wasn't supposed to work out like this, Oates had said. There were no prizes, any more, for guessing how it had been supposed to work out: the pseudo-ophiuroids had been supposed to become fully mature, fit for marriage and for war, Then, presumably, they had been expected to mate—but how, if the "fellows" were all identical, all the same sex, presumably "male" . . .

He wanted to demand responses to those speculations from Oates—but Oates was an officer, and a gentleman, not to mention a hero, as well as a pawn, and there was now a lady present, whose presence would inhibit any answers he might have to offer. Oates blinked—and Tom had never seen such a deliberate blink in his life. It seemed to him that Oates was blinking away the incipient horror that was in his eyes, in order that no one but Tom should see it; then he took a long sip of rum.

"Are you feeling ill, Captain Oates?" Helen asked. "You seem to be in distress."

"I'm sorry, Lady Anderley," Oates said, redirecting his gaze to Helen. "You caught me off guard for a moment. I sometimes still get shooting pains and wince. I should be grateful, I suppose—it reminds me how glad I ought to be that I'm alive . . . and getting better, thanks to you and Tom."

But a moment ago, Tom thought, *you told me that you were still dead.*

Tom had always been told that it took great courage to go over the top, to charge the enemy, but that had not been his experience—not after the first time, at any rate. What it had taken, for him, was something else entirely: resignation, desolation, an incapacity to care, a kind of madness. Sanity, he thought, would not have allowed him to do it a second time, but somehow, people could and did do it repeatedly; perhaps they had to go mad, but they could and did do that too. *Courage*, Tom thought, *is what it takes to sit at a dinner table in the presence of a friend, his wife and his child, and to keep a stiff upper lip, while you're absolutely sane, if not absolutely alive, and when something has gone wrong in a drama of which you're a part, although you don't want to be.*

Tom wasn't at all sure that he could have ever mustered that sort of courage—certainly not when he was Eton, or in Africa, and probably not now—but Titus could. He was cut from finer cloth than most men. He could sit upright, and move methodically, with hardly a tremor. He had eaten dinner—all four courses—without giving any sign of being under attack, save for a few trifling remarks slightly lacking in diplomacy. Tom measured, at that moment, the full extent of his friend's courage.

"I think Mercy would appreciate it if you'd look in on her, Tom," Helen said. "She was a little overexcited at dinner, because of the snow, and she's worried that she might have upset you, by mentioning your revolver . . . and the other thing."

"I didn't take it personally," Tom said. "I didn't know she'd seen the gun, but I took it out to the greenhouse anyway, to be on the safe side. As for what she said about the wounded men . . . well, it was simply true, wasn't it, and it shows uncommon sensitivity on her part to have realized it."

"You could tell her that," Helen said. "You could even kiss her goodnight, if you can steel yourself. She'd like that."

Tom glanced sideways at Oates, who seemed surprised to learn that such a suggestion was necessary.

"Now?" Tom asked, uncertainly.

"Now would be a good time," Helen said, firmly. "Don't worry about Captain Oates—I can keep him company for ten minutes or so. I have a couple of questions that I'd like to ask him, in private.

Tom wanted to protest, but couldn't think of any grounds on which he could reasonably do so. He put down his glass, which wasn't empty, intending that as a signal that he would be back as soon as he could, and he left the room.

His mind was racing, not wondering what it was that Helen wanted to say to Oates in private, but working on what seemed to be the more urgent problem.

The pseudo-ophiuroids weren't ready, for war . . . and, perhaps also for marriage. They were still immature, incapable of self-defense, let alone attack. Did that mean that Oates would be called upon to defend them? Against what, and how?

And what might Oates' discreet saviors be able to do, if they weren't ready either, but felt obliged to act anyway, to force the furtherance of their plan, which was presently unfolding according to monad/human time rather than barrel-boy time, at a pace to which *they* weren't accustomed, and with which they might not be able to cope, no matter how awesomely powerful and awesomely horrible *they* and their enemies were.

They and their enemies, Tom thought. *Are we under attack? With what? Snow?*

He had to interrupt himself then in order to open Mercy's door. She was sitting on the bed, still fully dressed—although it was pitch dark outside, it wasn't very late, and she obviously wasn't tired. She was waiting for him.

"I'm sorry, Daddy," she said, in a dutiful fashion that made it obvious that she was following orders.

"For what, sweetheart?"

"For going into your bedroom when you weren't there. For finding your gun."

"There's nothing to apologize for, lovely. It's entirely my fault for leaving the gun where you might find it."

"And for saying what I said about wounded men. I didn't mean you." She was blushing at the lie.

"That's all right, Mercy. If you had meant me, it would only have been the truth, and it would have been perfectly all right for you to say it. I did think I'd failed, and I still do. We won the war, so people say, but in the last of the three serious battles in which I was involved, we lost badly. I couldn't do anything about that, and I didn't do anything wrong, except survive . . . but we lost. The new German tanks just ran right through our lines. We were lucky the Americans arrived soon afterwards, in order to repair the damage. People say that you should forget things like that and move on, but the truth is that you can't. Once something that bad has happened, you can never forget it, even if you have to pretend. So you have to try hard to make sure that bad things don't happen. You're very young to have had to learn that lesson, and perhaps you're too young to understand it . . . but what you said only proves that you do understand it, a little, and that does you credit. You did your bit, during the war, and that was good, and kind. I'm proud of you, and you should be proud of yourself."

"It was nothing," she said. "All I did was play ball, and not very well. The American said I was a great little pitcher, but he was just humoring me. I didn't do anything that wasn't easy, and nobody was trying to drop bombs or poison gas on me, or shoot me. You were the one who was a hero."

"All I did was duck, darling, and hope that the bullets wouldn't hit me and that the gas mask wouldn't choke me. I wasn't a hero. I couldn't have done what you did, and make those wounded men feel a little bit better. For that, you have to be a real hero, like your mother."

"What about Captain Oates?" she asked. "Everyone says that he was a hero—that he sacrificed his life in order to give his friends a chance to survive. But Janet doesn't seem sure, because he's still alive and they're not. And Captain Oates doesn't seem sure, either."

Tom had to think hard about how to reply to that, but in the end he settled for banality; he was, after all talking to a seven-year-old, albeit one more mature than her years. "Oates was definitely a hero," he said. "I wasn't with him in Scott's tent, but I was with him in Africa, first in the West Yorkshires and then in the dragoons. I saw him in action. Trust me, he's a hero, through and through."

On that note, he leaned forward and kissed her gently on the forehead. It wasn't as difficult as he had imagined, and she did seem grateful.

"Good night, poppet," he added. "Don't stay up too long, will you?"

"Good night, Daddy," she said, and lay down on the bed, seemingly content, although she didn't make a start on undressing herself.

Tom went back downstairs, and made his way back to the study door.

"Have you finished your private discussion?" he asked.

"Yes," said Helen, curtly. Her expression gave no hint as to whether she had found the answers to her questions satisfactory or not.

Tom glanced at Oates, who avoided his gaze and took a sip of rum.

"There's no point in interrogating the Captain," Helen said. "I've forbidden him to tell you what I asked him, and he's given me his word as a gentleman that he won't. Did you put Mercy's mind at rest?"

"I did my best," Tom said. "It might not have been very good."

"She's a very tolerant child," Helen said. "She'll forgive you if it wasn't."

She takes after her mother, Tom thought, and wondered whether it would be as easy to kiss Helen as it had turned out to be to kiss Mercy. He thought not, but knew that he would have to try it eventually, the sooner the better—ideally tonight.

"Would you like a drink, darling?" he said.

"Rum?" Helen queried. "No thanks. I have to talk to Janet about tomorrow's food, and to make a few contingency plans. The snow has stopped for the moment, but it's already left an inch or two on the ground, and the wind's still blowing—we haven't finished yet. Will I see you later?"

"Yes," said Tom, firmly, "you will. That's a promise."

She raised an eyebrow, perhaps indicating skepticism, but all she said was: "Until then," and left, closing the door behind her.

"I'm sorry about that, Titus," Tom said to Oates. "I had to do it."

"You have absolutely nothing for which to apologize, Linny," Oates said. "It's me who should be apologizing to you. My presence here is an embarrassment. I should never have stayed. I did have a choice, I think, but . . . I wanted to see you again. I didn't think about the effect it might have on your family. If I'd known . . ."

"You don't have anything for which to apologize either," Tom assured him. "I was glad to see you . . . very glad. It's done me good . . . and if it's been of benefit to you, I'm doubly glad." He parted the curtains in order to look out. "Helen's right," he added. "The snow has stopped. It was a false alarm." He drained his glass, thankful for the raw bite of the rum.

Oates looked him in the face, sending shivers down his spine, and he said: "I have to get back to the starspawn, Linny," he said. "You don't have to come. I'll bolt the door. You might do better to stay here, with Helen."

No," said Tom, positively. "If you're going back to the greenhouse, so am I. We can stay up all night, if necessary. I know I'm only a botanist, and that the things don't bear the slightest resemblance to plants any more, but I'm a scientist. If something is going to happen, I want to see it."

"That might not be wise, Tom," Oates said, a trifle reluctantly. "It might get ugly . . . and desperate. I don't think anything can come of it, but *in extremis* . . . I'll have to try."

"Yes, it is wise," Tom said. "There's no wisdom without careful observation, but if things get ugly, *in extremis* . . . that I need to see. And haven't you just given Helen your word as a gentleman to look after me, as best you can? You can't do that if you're there and I'm here?"

Oates looked startled. Evidently, he had given Helen exactly that promise, but he had also given her his word not to tell Tom, and the promise still bound him, even if Tom had already guessed. Instead he said: "I fear that it might be a matter of you trying to look after me, Tom," he said, using his friend's name instead of his nickname for a second time, to emphasize how far they had come from Eton, "but you can't. Trust me—you *can't.*"

"We'll see," said Tom. "It's about time that I had a chance to repay a little of that particular debt. Let's go."

Oates shook his head, but raised no further objection.

When he stepped out of the side door of the manor, Tom paused to pick up a handful of snow from a four-inch drift beside the doorstep, which was still soft and fluffy.

"It's just snow," he said to Oates. "Ordinary snow."

"Good," said Oates. "Let's hope it stays that way."

Tom didn't ask him to explain, suspecting that he wouldn't be able to do so. He didn't have a clue regarding what kind of barrage was going to come down, but he knew that he had to face it alongside Oates. They were in it together, for better or for worse. They didn't have to understand it, but they did have to do it. They weren't ready, evidently, but they had to do it anyway. Something wicked, it appeared, might be coming their way. Oates clearly didn't know exactly what it was any more than Tom did, but he had a feeling: a pricking in his thumbs, or something equivalent. That was enough.

Tom had a feeling too, but it was more akin to something stirring in his heart. He was glad of that, because his heart had been inert for a long time, and it was good to know that he wouldn't have to stab himself with a bayonet to discover whether he was still capable of feeling.

The wind was bitter, and becoming furious. A few belated clusters of snowflakes, whipped up from the ground, seemed to be coming at them horizontally, from the right. Tom was glad that they didn't have to slog into the teeth of the wind to reach the palace of golden light that was beckoning to him from the Stygian gloom.

Tom was not at all clear in his mind as to who he ought to be rooting for if he was, in fact, to be caught up in a war. Were Tweedledum and Tweedledee, the famous vampire starfish, a potential enemy, or were he and they now allies against evil Arcticans? Was he in one of those situations where the enemy of his enemy might be his friend, or one of those situations in which he had no friends, and in which anyone in the crossfire between rival factions was likely to be ripped apart no matter how the real contest worked out?

X

TOM went into the greenhouse a few yards ahead of Oates, who was catching snowflakes in his hand and peering at them. They were beginning to descend thickly again. Tom didn't hold the door for him, because his eyes had immediately gone to the troughs where the pseudo-ophiuroids were supposed to be, still partly-buried in artificial wombs of bloody soil, peeping out warily, either at this world or another.

The two that were in advance of the others weren't in the mangers, but they weren't hard to spot.

They didn't look much like echinoderms any more.

They were hanging from the branches of the poor male banana tree, like vast spiders' webs in an orchard, brought into temporary visibility by morning dew.

They had stretched . . . no, not stretched, Tom corrected himself . . . they had *unraveled*—partially, at least. The tightly-wound fibers of which they were composed had loosened and expanded, without becoming any less labyrinthine. They were more intricate now than anything Tom had ever seen or imagined, and their folds and coils and their intermittent tangles had become strangely blurred, giving the impression that they extended into more dimensions than the visible three, that they were actively reaching out into extraordinary spaces.

The tree was visibly dying. It was perhaps the only male banana tree in England, and it was dying from contact with the aliens, or perhaps with the dimension into which they were reaching.

However absurd the sensation might have been, Tom felt angry on the tree's behalf. He could have taken it more easily if it had been one of the pineapple trees, or even one of the female banana trees.

He looked back at Oates, intending to ask for an explanation—but the other didn't say a word. He was inside the greenhouse now, having closed the door behind him, trying to brush a few clinging snowflakes off his clothing. There were not many; although the snow was falling densely now, Oates had got inside before the soft and silent storm had reached its peak. He was not making much progress in clearing his jacket; the flakes, which ought to have melted almost instantly in the torrid ambient temperature of the greenhouse, were still sparkling stubbornly, and Oates' movements were becoming increasingly urgent. He gave every indication of being a man in desperate conflict with himself, fighting for control of his own limbs—and his own face.

It seemed to Tom that Oates' features were attempting to bloat and blur again, to resume the hideousness that had possessed them when he had first confronted Tom on the driveway, but that Oates was fighting back, trying to hold himself together, to maintain his identity and his integrity. The objective of the assault, however, was not to alter his features; that was only a side-effect. The real problem was more fundamental, more deep-seated. Something inside him was trying to make him do something, but Oates was determined not to do it.

That interpretation of what was happening was only based on a subjective impression, but it was aided by its context. It was the only hint that Tom needed in order to jump to the conclusion of the conundrum that Oates had posed him earlier: what did he know that he didn't know that he knew? Mentally, Tom slotted the pieces of the puzzle together.

Something, he concluded, really was inside Oates: an ingenious filamental endoparasite hitching a ride through the subterranean labyrinth to Andersley; a discreet and prudent endoparasite, but an endoparasite with a purpose, perhaps not devoid of a certain intelligence.

As to what that purpose might be, Tom was less certain, but there was one possibility that stuck out like a sore thumb, because it would provide an answer to a question he had posed himself only a few moments before. Tweedledum and Tweedledee were not ready, for marriage or for war, but even if they had been fully mature, they were both male. If the intention of nurturing them in the greenhouse had been to prepare them to mate with a "female," exactly as the rare male banana tree had been carefully maintained in order to fertilize much more abundant females kept for "bearing fruit," then a female would have to come to meet them . . . and would likely come even if the chances of a fertile encounter seemed slim, because any remote chance would be better than none . . .

Tom wanted desperately to help Oates, but he didn't know what to do, and Oates was clearly incapable of telling him, or even of giving him a hint. The stray snowflakes were beginning falling off his jacket, though, and although the remaining flakes weren't melting in the heat, they were changing, losing their whiteness and their brightness.

Tom felt a chill run down his spine. He had no way of knowing whether he might have been biologically contaminated by the pseudo-ophiuroids while handling their "seeds" with unprotected hands before "planting them." In any case, he had been living in close company with Oates every day, breathing the same humid air in and out. The possibility that he was incubating some kind of infection, unobtrusive thus far, certainly could not be ruled out, no matter how reluctant he might be to believe it.

For the first time, but without any real sense of surprise, Tom felt that something was *reaching out* to him, trying to get some sort of grip on him. He felt his toes and fingers beginning to tingle, and his heart rate increasing.

He fought the sensation, and felt that he was winning, but that it was conquerable.

He felt that he had to do something active, that he needed to assert and confirm his authority over his own body, and his own mind. Even though he had only the vaguest idea what was happening, he felt that he had to react, because it was obvious that some kind of climax was developing in the greenhouse, and he wanted to be able to take a hand in it. He was still a soldier, in spite of having resigned from that profession twice, and in spite of the psychological catastrophe that had come to a head on the Chemin des Dames. He did what any soldier would have done, and reached for his gun, which was in a drawer in the table, within arm's reach of the spot where he was standing. There were bullets scattered in the drawer, and he swiftly inserted three in the cylinder and rotated it so that one of them was under the hammer.

Even as he did that, though, almost automatically, Tom was struck by the thought of how utterly absurd the reflex was. Was he going to *shoot* two monstrous cobwebs? How on Earth—or even on the edge of the Earth, on the borderlands of the labyrinth and the world of the Other Antarctica—could he expect mere bullets to have any effect? Filamental flesh was unlike cellular flesh. Perhaps the threads could be torn, but was it not likely that they had evolved in such a fashion as to be adaptable to impact, resilient to penetration?

He had turned away from Oates in order to pick up the gun, and he was looking at the poor dying banana tree again, still furious on behalf of his cherished specimen.

He raised the revolver in order to direct it against the nearer of the vampires, even though he knew that it might just as well have been a crucifix: a symbol absurdly out of context, hardly meaningful to him, and not at all meaningful to *them*.

He was helpless, and knew it. He didn't squeeze the trigger.

Instead, he turned his head again to look at Oates, hoping for some inspiration, some guidance, some spark of understanding—but what he got was a bad dream, the substance of night terrors even worse than those he had been nurturing ever since his return from France.

Oates' face now seemed tortured out of all recognition, even though it was made of the same familiar flesh. It seemed to Tom that it was no longer a face at all, but a shadow of a face: a mask applied over something unhuman. Tom looked at where his friend's eyes should have been, but all he could see, for the moment, was alien darkness, with the suggestion of cyclopean buildings in the distance.

It's not real, he told himself. *It's a delusion.* He thought that it was probably true—even that it had to be true, rationally—but he could not convince himself. He was *seeing*; what he was seeing was on the very edge of the reality that was normally visible to his untrained eyes, and hence incomprehensible but it was no mere illusion.

It seemed to Tom that he was looking into the very heart of madness, and suddenly, strangely, the meaning of the oddly nonsensical phrase that Oates had pronounced—beyond the mountains of madness—lost its oddity and its nonsensicality. Tom was now in a different world, where different vocabularies were required for description and thought. Mentally, he was in the labyrinth, already in danger of losing his way, with no guiding thread.

Oates still seemed to be fighting, with every fiber of his flesh and every ounce of his will-power, but his arms were no longer flailing at the fake snowflakes remaining on his jacket, which had lost every hint of whiteness. He had torn the jacket open, snapping the thread of the buttons, and he was clawing at the shirt underneath, ripping the cotton, and even tearing at the skin underneath with his fingernails, drawing blood.

Tom felt sure that his friend was trying to stop what he was doing, but that he couldn't. He didn't understand what his friend was attempting to do, but he knew that the poor fellow would never be able to dig a hole through his ribs with his fingernails.

He didn't have to. While Oates was working away at his chest from one side, impotently, something else was working from the other side, more clinically and more effectively, not cutting through the ribs but somehow *dissolving* them.

A hole appeared in Oates' bare and bloody chest, and expanded, like a dilating pupil, to reveal the same crazed darkness that was visible in the orbits of his eyes within the cavity of his chest, where his heart and lungs ought to be—and evidently still were, Tom's scientific mind informed him, since his body was still moving. The alien darkness had not replaced his viscera, but was merely sharing their location, their space. As he stared into that darkness, Tom obtained the same suggestion of distant architectures, lost in time and space.

It's quite real, he told himself, deliberately reversing his earlier judgment. *It doesn't make sense, in my conceptual framework, but I'm just a poor ignoramus who only knows one word for snow. It's real, it's material, and it's not beyond reach. Indeed, all the evidence says that it's discreet, prudent, insidious . . . and therefore must be vulnerable. It's not supernatural, and even though it's the stuff of which dreams are made, in the final analysis, it's still* stuff. *The pseudo-ophiuroids really are naturally endoparasitic, and their original hosts really were giants of some kind . . . monsters . . . but they've fallen on evolutionary hard times, survivors of some distant catastrophe.*

Something pulled itself out of the impossible void, through the gap in Oates' ribs.

He didn't collapse. Oates had a gaping hole in his chest, but he didn't collapse. Blood was trickling from the edges, but not gushing from severed blood-vessels. Tom had seen men with holes blasted in their chests before, but Oates' wound was not as catastrophic, in spite of its dimensions. Oates was still standing, still wrestling with himself as the flexible pseudo-ophiuroid squeezed through the fissure in his being.

Prudent parasites, Tom reminded himself, *don't kill their prey, even when the time comes to decamp. The perfect parasite is one that preserves its host, keeps its host healthy. Natural selection picks out the parasites that do the least permanent damage—and in the fullness of time, given millions or billions of years, it picks out the parasites that make a positive contribution to their hosts' wellbeing. All parasites tend, in the long run, to evolve toward the condition of symbionts. That has only happened rarely on Earth, but Earth is a very primitive world, in the cosmic scheme of things. Colonists wanting to make it a land fit for their own heroes who would have a long job on their hands.*

217

Oates was still standing up, and his movements were becoming less agitated. As the endosparasite made its exit, his face began to return to what Tom still thought of as "normal": Oates' own face, as he remembered it from long ago, from before the Terra Nova expedition. The madness was leaking from his inner being, and the void in his chest was already no longer a void. Tom could now see Oates' beating heart within the hole. Oates could see it too, as he looked down at his ruined clothes, his oozing blood, and the thing that was crawling out of him.

Unsurprisingly, it bore some slight resemblance to a starfish, or rather to an ophiuroid, with five long flexible arms and fists tufted with hairs, and little eye-stalks peeping curiously, perhaps trying to adjust the vision of their little black orbs to a world of light, air, warmth and humidity. It was wet and bright, richly filled with blood—Oates' blood—and it didn't seem to know exactly where to go, or how to get there, but it was clearly impelled by a need to go somewhere. It dangled from Oates;' stubbornly upright torso, and let itself down on to the floor. There, it began to squirm, crawling over the moist tiled floor much as an actual ophiuroid would have made its way over the sea-bed. However alien its flesh might be, it was subject to the same principles of biodynamics, the same logic of design.

Oates watched it go, standing very still, as if he dared not move while he had that gaping hole in his chest, in case his heart fell out.

The hole was closing again, though; the dissolved ribs were already regenerating. Oates seemed to be holding his breath, waiting, perhaps knowing that he would have to wait for the pleural cavity to seal itself up before he could breathe properly again. His parasite belonged to a very prudent species, it seemed, perhaps even a generous one . . . or perhaps Oates was still needed, for further duties in the service of his aspirant symbiont . . . military service, given that it was at war, oppressed by an Arctican weapon that resembled snow

In the meantime, the vampire starfish that had been living inside Oates for weeks, and perhaps for seven years, was squirming on. It was definitely heading for its companions, but it would have to get past Tom in order to get to the banana tree. Tom wondered—because rather than in spite of the chill within him that seemed to be trying to freeze his heart and limbs—whether he ought to try to stop it. He had been nurturing the alien organisms for weeks, but he could not help thinking that it might now be too dangerous to nurture them any longer, no matter what the cost of his betraying them might be to poor Oates.

Is it the snow that's chilling me? he wondered. *Oates was able to fight it, so I ought to be able to fight it too. Only a few flakes landed on my face, and I hardly felt their impact, but I didn't make the slightest attempt to brush them away. Perhaps they've been absorbed into my flesh and I've been conscripted into the war . . . but I can still fight. Should I?*

He was confused, not knowing where in the alien war his sympathies ought to lie. If his interpretation of the situation were correct, then the thing that had been inside Oates—which had apparently done him no mortal harm, even while making its horrible exit from his torso—was merely making a desperate heroic effort, against long odds, to reach its intended mate. Had things worked out as intended, that exit might not have been necessary, at least in the greenhouse. Oates might have been able to carry the mature pseudo-ophiuroids back into the labyrinth, and Tom would never have known what had become of his friend.

On the other hand . . . it was the Arcticans who were attacking, subtly but perhaps savagely, and Tom's first impulse was to defend the creatures that had saved his friend's life, the creatures that his friend had found beautiful . . .

Helplessly, he looked at Oates for guidance, hoping to see something in his expression, something in his eyes, other than darkness.

And he did. Now that he was free of the awful physical intimacy of his endoparasite, Oates' mind was free of its subtle censorship. His body was not yet capable of any violent movement; he could not take action himself . . . but Oates met Tom's gaze, and seemed to Tom to be imploring him to act in his stead. And abruptly, Tom made his decision. He had no way of knowing which side he ought to be on, in the context of the World War, but he felt that he needed to act, that he needed to *play the hero*.

Tom took three strides and reached out with his left hand toward the tap controlling the gas supply to the heaters. That hand suddenly felt very cold indeed, but with stern determination—fighting for himself, he thought—he completed the action. The gas jets under the floor went out. The door wasn't open, because Oates had closed it when he had lurched in, and Tom knew that the temperature wouldn't drop very rapidly—but drop it would.

He lowered the hand holding the gun then, and took aim at the squirming thing on the floor. His scientific mind couldn't help noticing that it was definitely not identical to Tweedledum and Tweedledee. It was the same species, but it was a different morph. The aliens *did* have sex, he concluded, confirming his initial speculation: just two of them, much like humans and other earthly creatures, but two was enough . . . more than enough in circumstances in which a domesticated species could be exploited, as part of a project of colonization . . . until things went awry.

Tom felt increasingly sure of what he now knew, or thought that he knew. The barrel-boys were great cultivators, true sons of Cain. The pseudo-ophiuroids, whose usual far-from-natural habitat was indeed inside another of their slave species, forming an artificial hybrid therewith—a minotaur—were the barrel-boys' bananas, almost all "female," and the "males" of the species had been neglected, to the point of near-extinction . . . save for a few seed-specimens kept in cold storage, just in case it ever became politic, or necessary, to reintroduce the kind of variability that sexual reproduction could provide into the domesticated species. But in order to do that, the conditions necessary to their development had to be duplicated, or faked, and the specimens had to be brought to maturity, in order to have intercourse, in order to breed.

An organism, Tom knew, as a biologist, was simply a seed's ingenious way of producing more seeds, or an egg's ingenious way of producing more eggs—and the process was necessarily slow.

But the creatures from beyond the mountains of madness weren't ready. Oates had not known, consciously, what he was doing, save for a few vague suspicions that had crept into his dreams, but he had known that his charges were not yet ready . . . for marriage or for war.

Tom knew, now—or thought he knew—what the barrel-boys were doing. They had nothing against human beings; they had no interest in taking over the human world—their priorities lay elsewhere. Humans, to them, were just innocent bystanders, of no strategic interest, unless they somehow became useful. Cattle bore only the slightest resemblance to the original hosts of the vampire starfish, not even being made of the same kind of flesh, but convergent evolution by natural selection produced similar organic compounds within their bodies to perform similar organic functions. Ox-blood was not the blood on which the pseudo-ophiuroids had once fed in their natural environment—it probably bore no more resemblance to it than Camp Coffee to real coffee—but it would do, in a pinch, in order to permit the vampire starfish to proliferate variably . . . and there would be time, once they had begun to proliferate in that fashion, to make better and more permanent provision. And if the supply of ox-blood proved to be inadequate to a sufficiently rapid proliferation, there were other organisms of a similar type available . . .

The Arcticans had no interest in humans either, Tom presumed, and certainly no moral concern for them. They just wanted to throw a spanner into the works of whatever long-term plan the barrel-boys were hatching. For the moment, though, the snow seemed to him to be on the side of the angels of Mons, covering Andersley and covering the human retreat from the battle that had not even properly begun.

The alien ophiuroids weren't ready for sex, evidently, but the would-be mother was going for it anyway, in circumstances that were very far from ideal, but impelled by a primal drive, and perhaps with some chance of success, if the pseudo-ophiuroids were able to complete their meeting of bodies and minds, fusing their unimaginable complex webs. Perhaps, from their point of view, it was one of those million-to-one shots so common in earthly popular fiction, which just might work. Tom couldn't tell—but one thing of which he was sure was that he was still in the way.

He fired the gun.

At least, he tried to fire it, but he found that couldn't squeeze the trigger. It was as if the temperature of his hand had suddenly dropped by a hundred degrees and frostbite had seized his fingers. His hand was incapable of movement, stuck hard to the butt of the gun, but incapable of pulling the trigger. The gun itself seemed to have been locked solid, perhaps because all the humidity in the air had momentarily condensed into ice. For the moment, the idea surged forth within his mind, that the weapon couldn't fire. It was useless. So was he.

Tom realized that the alien war wasn't just raging around him, but inside him. It had been foolish to think, even for an instant, that he might not have been contaminated by the alien biology, that its agents hadn't been lurking inside him for weeks, prudently, in the form of invisible microbes . . . but microbes capable of coming together, if necessary, of fusing their multitudinous filaments into ingenious fibers

Tom tried to raise his foot, intending to stamp on the squirming thing—which was by no means fast-moving, even though it had to be going as rapidly as it could.

He couldn't do that, either. He was frozen to the spot, like a statue—probably not literally, but psychologically.

The squirming thing began to climb up his body—not, he assumed, because it was going to dig a hole in his chest and take up residence in the pleural cavity, wrapped around his heart, but because it was going to use him as a ladder to get to its inamorata-to-be. He knew that when it got to his arms—including the one whose hand was clutching the temporarily-useless gun—he would have to be unfrozen, at least partially. He would have to be able to turn around, and to pass the parasite that had crawled out of Oates' body into the branches of the dead tree. where its eager lovers were waiting . . . and he suspected that it probably wouldn't want him to turn away again thereafter, for modesty's sake.

But he could fight. His mind was still working, still possessed of free will. He was capable of action, if he could only think of some useful action and carry it out, before the creatures within him—the discreet, prudent parasites—could move to stop him. It was still possible to stop the pseudo-ophiuroid female making her attempt to copulate with the young males that were, in theory, unready, but might, in practice, be fertile . . .

As to what might happen afterwards . . .

The alien life hadn't yet been able to possess Tom, in the way that it had possessed Oates. It had only been able to get into him, psychologically and physically, to the extent of being about to send a few shivers down his spine and a touch of pseudo-frostbite to his fingers. It wasn't very powerful; it could be fought; it had taken him by surprise, but he was a scientist, and he ought to be able to work out what he could still do—and to do it. He felt that he had to stop the vampire starfish from completing their maneuver, not for his own sake, but to alleviate the more distant threat to his livestock, and to Helen and the servants, to the farmers and the estate workers, to Yorkshire . . . and above all, to Mercy.

Mercy! he thought.

And suddenly, as if it were a word of power, even unspoken, there she was, in the doorway of the golden palace—the door to which she had just opened, because Oates had neglected to bolt it—with a snowball in her hand.

She threw it, without an instant's delay.

She threw it at Tom, purely for fun, purely as a game, motivated by the thrill of being naughty, of having slipped out of the house by night in order to play in the snow, encouraged in that tactical disobedience because he had gone to see her in her room, in order to reassure her that he was not annoyed with her, that he really did love her unconditionally, in spite of his recent coldness.

She threw the snowball at Tom, therefore, for complicated, tangled reasons. It was probably a coincidence that she threw it directly at the thing that was climbing up his body, which she could not have seen clearly, and could not have understood on the basis of what she was seeing.

She was seven years old. She threw like a little girl— but she threw like a little girl who had played ball on the lawn with wounded soldiers in order to reintroduce them to the pleasure of play: a little girl who had *done her bit*. She threw the snowball like a practiced hero.

The projectile couldn't possibly have hurt the monster with the impact of its mass, no matter how warm the monster liked its environment to be, if it had really been a mere snowball. But it wasn't a *mere* snowball. It was what Oates' passenger had been worried about when he first looked up at the glass roof. His endoparasite hadn't been anxious about the snow as such; it had been worried about the possibility that some of the snowflakes weren't really snowflakes, that there might be something else riding the snowstorm.

And there was.

Perhaps Mercy had found it entirely by accident, having slipped out to play regardless of parental orders. Tom preferred that hypothesis to the possibility that even before she had formed the soft snow into a compact ball, enough of the fake flakes had been absorbed by her flesh for the infection to be able to influence her, to nudge her in the desired direction. He hoped, earnestly, that the snow hadn't been able to get inside her, hadn't helped her make up her mind what she was going to do with the snowball. He believed, firmly, that it was her own idea, her own work. She was a hero. She had always intended to throw the snowball at her father, and she thought that the thing crawling up his body was just a target, conveniently placed by chance.

She was a great little pitcher. The snowball hit the squirming thing that was squirming up Tom's abdomen fair and square: a perfect strike—and suddenly, it found the capacity to squirm much more urgently than before.

It lost its grip. It fell—and it went on writhing. It wasn't dead, though—not by a long chalk. And the two that were hanging on the banana tree, which weren't injured at all, began to squirm too, in order to come to meet it. Tom's suddenly-unfrozen hands were already reaching out to grasp them, as if to help them down, to help them come together.

But his mind was still his own. He still had free will. If the tiny things inside him could motivate his muscles, so could he. He was still himself, still a soldier. He was an officer, it was not his function simply to do, but to understand, if understanding was humanly possible. And he thought that, for once, he *did* understand. He was capable not merely of doing but of knowing what he was doing, and why he was doing it—and he did it.

He had *presence of mind*, in a way that he had not had for some considerable time, not because of anything the aliens had done to him, but simply because of his own shell-shocked incapacity

He jerked his right hand upwards and squeezed the trigger of the revolver that it was still holding—and the trigger worked. Even if it were not illusory, the ice that seemed to have frozen the gun's mechanism was already melting, already liquefying, perhaps partly because of the warmth still contained in the atmosphere of the greenhouse, and partly because of the warmth that had abruptly been returned to Tom's hand. The gun fired— not at the webs hanging on the banana tree but at the glass panes of the roof above them.

In the few hours that had elapsed since he and Oates had left the greenhouse in order to go to dinner, the outer surface of the glass had cooled dramatically, and the snow had begun to pile up there in spite of the wind, from which the relevant panes were sheltered by a flue-stack.

Hit by bullets, the panes shattered, and multitudinous shards of glass fell. Tom ducked reflexively in order to avoid the bombardment, and the shower only inflicted a few small cuts on his scalp. The snow that had piled up on the glass, however, wasn't just snow. It came down like a small avalanche to begin with, followed by a gentle rain of soft clustered flakes.

The real snow in the mixture was melting even as it fell, even though the temperature was declining steadily, but the unsnow wasn't melting with it; it was resistant to warmth. Plainly, the creatures from the Other Antarctica had some resistance to it. They fought back, but they were now outnumbered and outgunned. They were no more ready for a fight than they had been for marriage. They didn't stand a chance, any more than the makeshift battalions of exhausted walking wounded assembled on the Chemin des Dames in '18 had stood a chance against the surging tanks.

The fake snowflakes had to consist of a dedicated toxin, Tom thought: a carefully-designed pesticide. The fake snow was light-years ahead of mustard-gas-oozing shells, but it was a refinement of the same supposedly-sophisticated kind of warfare. It had probably been in cold storage for millions of years, but it still worked.

As Tom rubbed the snowflakes that had fallen on his own head into his bleeding scalp and his cheeks, he thought about Sir John Franklin, and all the Arctic explorers who had gone to search for him, and all of those bodies that had never been found during the decades. Perhaps, he thought, some of them had fallen into crevasses, and perhaps more than one of the crevasses had been traps, and perhaps something millions of billions of years old—far older than the legendary Hyperborea—was still lurking underneath and in parallel with the ice of the Arctic Ocean and its Arctic islands. Perhaps Oates wasn't the first human conscript into the slow, cold World War . . . in which case, he surely wouldn't be the last.

One thing that was certain, though, Tom thought, was that the colonial war hadn't ended. Its warriors weren't mayflies. They took a much longer view than Earl Haig and Ludendorff . . . but that didn't necessarily mean that their strategy was any better, that they were not, in the final analogical analysis, donkeys.

The webs on the dead banana tree were shriveling— not for want of blood or heat, but because they'd been blasted, gassed, shell-shocked . . . killed. The writhing thing on the floor at Tom's feet was still writhing, but the hectic movements were its death-throes. It wasn't going anywhere. Neither were the immature vampire starfish, which were already dissolving in their troughs.

But the story hadn't ended yet.

Tom looked at Oates, who was still looking down with frank astonishment at his lacerated but almost-healed torso and the blood that was no longer flowing in such profusion. Almost immediately, Oates raised his head in order to meet Tom's gaze. Tom looked into his eyes—Oates' own eyes, the frank eyes of a good friend, without the slightest shadow about them—and he could see that Oates wasn't ready to fall over, that the light of intelligence wasn't about to go out. Oates was alive, probably for the second time, but alive nevertheless and still his old self, still Captain Lawrence Oates, still a hero—but he had a more intimate and more complex connection to the inhabitants of the Other World than Tom. He had free will, but he wasn't *completely* free. He was still a prisoner of war, restricted in his movements, in his dreams, and to some extent in his thoughts.

"Titus . . ." said Tom.

"They weren't ready," Oates whispered—and this time he added: "Thank God." He too had glimpsed the further possibilities of the barrel-boys' project. He too had decided, as best he could on the evidence available to him, on which side he would rather be. Whether he would be punished for that or not, Tom could only hazard a guess, but his actual and speculative acquaintance with creatures ambitious to play god did not fill him with confidence . . . quite the reverse.

Oates looked into Tom's eyes, with an expression that combined affection, and longing, and also apology, although he really had nothing at all for which to apologize . . .

"I'm just going to step outside, Linny," he said, with a quiet and utterly heroic dignity, carefully deleting any expletives that might have sprung to mind. "I might be gone for some time." The door was still open. Oates went through it and disappeared into the desultory snowstorm, presumably not in search of a crevasse. His legs were sound and he could doubtless have limped for miles, but Tom did not think that he would have to go that far before being claimed by the labyrinth.

Tom picked Mercy up just as Helen arrived in the doorway through which Oates had gone—chasing after her daughter, as she often did, but far too late, as usual, to prevent her from going where had she wanted to go. She was followed by Janet, who was carrying a Zulu spear from one of the Old Earl's panoplies in the unused drawing room, which she had doubtless grabbed after hearing the gunshots and the shattering glass. She was ready to do her bit, if required, however poorly equipped she was.

Tom clutched Mercy to him, kissing her persistently and repeatedly on the forehead and the cheeks. Taken by surprise, she was squirming reflexively, trying to evade his unprecedented insistence. He had already dropped the gun, and his right hand was free to reach out and invite Helen into the collective embrace. Her reflexes worked differently, and she didn't hesitate to submit to the attraction, in spite of the inexplicable chaos around them.

Tom was weeping, but he didn't consider that to be conduct unbecoming an officer, given the circumstances. Quite the opposite, in fact. He took his wife and daughter out of the greenhouse, and Janet followed them, still holding the spear in both hands, ready for defensive deployment. Tom switched off the lights as he went, and closed the door behind him, but he didn't seal the padlock.

"What about the breadfruit?" Helen asked, having taken note of the fact that the heating was off.

"They'll survive for one night," he said, as he went into the house through the kitchen door, where Maggie and Beth were standing, peering out curiously into the snow. "They're tough enough for that. They're native to Earth, after all. Pity about the male banana tree, though. They're rare."

Tom took his wife and daughter into the study, where he sat them down, giving Mercy pride of place in what he had recently come to think of as "Oates' armchair."

"I'm sorry," Mercy said, automatically.

"That's all right, Mercy," Tom said, "but in future, do as you're told."

"I will," she lied.

"Is it over?" Helen asked.

"No," said Tom. "It will never be over. That wasn't even a skirmish, let alone a battle. The barrel-boys are still dug in, more deeply entrenched than we can imagine, and so are their enemies. The stalemate might well be unbreakable, at least within the lifetime of our species. We don't even know for sure whether we pitched in on the right side. The barrel-boys probably think of the ophiuroids as symbionts, whose fusion with an earthly species would represent an improvement beneficial to everyone, an evolutionary forward leap for life as we know it. They might well think that I'm an ingrate or a coward, and that I should have followed Oates . . . but they don't seem to be putting any pressure on me, for the moment."

"He hasn't come back to the house," Helen observed, tentatively.

"No," said Tom. "I doubt that he will. If we ever see him again, it probably won't be for some considerable time."

"That's a shame," Mercy put in. "Even though he wouldn't play with me, and kept you in the greenhouse all day long, I liked him being here."

"So did I," said Tom, "but without him, things will soon settle back into the old routine."

Helen frowned at that, but didn't protest. Instead, she turned to Mercy. "It's high time you were in bed, poppet," she said. "I'll come upstairs with you, but this time, you need to go to bed for real, and go to sleep like a good girl."

"I will," Mercy promised. "I can always make more snowballs tomorrow."

"So you can," said Helen, taking her by the hand. In the doorway, she stopped and looked back at Tom.

"That promise you made still stands," she said. "And I have a *lot* of questions to ask you."

"I'm sure you do," said Tom, "but I hope I can supply some of the answers, now."

He was perfectly sincere. He hoped. He had lost that capability, for a while, but he had found it again now, and was glad of it. What had life to offer that was more precious? What else, in fact, had life, however labyrinthine, ever had to offer?